T0155086

For Keepsies

For Keepsies

STORIES BY GARY FINCKE

COFFEE HOUSE PRESS :: MINNEAPOLIS :: 1993

Some of these stories first appeared in the following magazines: "Story Stories" in *Hayden's Ferry Review*, "For Keepsies" in *Minnesota Review*, "Six Letters, Starting with E," "On the Radio," and "My Father Told Me," in the *Beloit Fiction Journal*, "The Underground House" in *South Carolina Review*, "The Man Who Played for the Skyliner" in *Florida Review*, "Grade Nine" and "The Nazi on the Phone," in *Cimarron Review*, "Tinderbox" in *New Mexico Humanities Review*.

The publishers would like to thank the following funders for assistance that helped make this book possible: the Bush Foundation; Dayton Hudson Foundation on behalf of Dayton's and Target Stores; The General Mills Foundation; The National Endowment for the Arts, A federal agency; The Jerome Foundation; The Lannan Foundation; The Andrew W. Mellon Foundation; The Beverly J. and John A. Rollwagen Fund of the Minneapolis Foundation; Star Tribune/Cowles Media Company; and The McKnight Foundation. This activity is made possible in part by a grant provided by the Minnesota State Arts Board, through an appropriation by the Minnesota State Legislature. Major new marketing initiatives have been made possible by the Lila Wallace-Reader's Digest Literary Publishers Marketing Development Program, funded through a grant to the Council of Literary Magazines and Presses.

Coffee House Press books are available to the trade through our primary distributor, Consortium Book Sales & Distribution, 1045 Westgate Drive, Saint Paul, MN 55114. Our books are also available through all major library distributors and jobbers, and through most small press distributors, including Bookpeople, Inland, and Small Press Distribution. For personal orders, catalogs or other information, write to: Coffee House Press 27 North Fourth Street, Suite 400, Minneapolis, MN 55401.

library of congress cip data
Fincke, Gary.
For Keepsies : stories / by Gary Fincke.
p.   cm.
contents: The Nazi on the phone—For Keepsies—The underground house—On the radio—Tinderbox—Grade nine—Six letters starting with E— The man who played for the Skyliners—The Aqua-velva man—My father told me.
ISBN 1-56689-013-6
1. Title.
PS3556.I457F67   1993
813'.54—dc20   93-2457
                                                      CIP

Contents

The Nazi on the Phone

"Hhaaah," Carol Dawson said at the end of every yawn. *Hhaaah*, as if yawns were sneezes, audible bursts of breath that deserved something like "God bless you." Fifteen minutes didn't go by without Carol yawning. *Hhaaah*. You could count on it, a kind of simple-minded, one-note carillon that told you life was getting shorter.

Maybe she was perpetually tired. Or anxious. Maybe she'd lapsed into a stupid habit, vocalizing her yawns the way some people nail-bite or ear-tug. What I didn't do was ask her its origin the whole summer of 1970 when I stayed with the Dawsons three nights a week because my high school friend Dick, her husband, ended up, like me, doing graduate work at Kent State University six years after we'd left Pittsburgh behind.

It was better than driving back and forth, four days a week, to my apartment seventy miles east. It was better than renting. And I'd already learned what coincidence was before the summer began, standing around gawking at Kent State's plunge into history as if I were one of those benign faces you see on the television news, the ones looking at the camera and the candidate while a gun pokes out of the crowd an arm's length from where we're gaping.

And every time I think of watching the guardsmen kneel and fire, I hear Carol Dawson go *Hhaaah*, as if she hadn't slept in weeks or was giving the code-sound for *Why didn't they shoot you, too, while they had the chance?*

I knew our eleven seconds on the firing line was *history*. It hadn't just rippled through the newspapers with the peristaltic motion of the news, front page to back, a few bumps along the way to remind you what things had looked like in their undigested state. By mid-summer the Student Unrest Commission had set up shop in Kent, and now all the accidental witnesses like me were being drawn over the mountains of our memories to see what we could see.

And so Dick and I listened to a self-interest catalogue of theories: from conspiracy to snipers to terrorists to murder to convergence of the planets. It was like hearing Nixon explain the powder burns on his hands from his *Bums* speech, the one he'd been so proud to deliver on May 1 because it told people what they wanted to hear about students like Dick Dawson and me who milked 2-s deferments for graduate school—we were the reason this country had hit the skids like a Third World Goon Squad.

"Christ," Dick said after we sat through those first sessions, "they could have wrapped this up months ago. They could have put the guardsmen up there where they belong and grilled the fucking truth out of them."

"Sure," I answered, as if I were agreeing with my Middle English professor after I hadn't read any of the secondary work for class.

"They're putting housewives on the stand. They're in-
terviewing landlords and shopkeepers. They're letting
Del Corso break out the sniper theory again. It's like
listening to a lecture by the Flat Earth Society."

"They're putting their fingers on the pulse," I said, but
Dick wasn't through.

"They're letting Mayor Satrom talk tomorrow. We'll
get the 'Anarchy in Portage County' speech again."

"Brought to you by the same people who send you all
that fellowship money," I said, though I wondered
where my subpoena was.

Dick kept all the articles from the *Akron Beacon Journal* in his bedroom and had a file on everything. He had
a hundred pictures he'd taken on May 2, May 3, and May
5. He grilled me a dozen times, and at the end of every
session, after we watched the slides again, he told me the
biggest regret of his life was that he hadn't been on campus on May 4. "Who would have thought it was coming?" he said each time, and I had to agree. I hadn't
thought anything was coming except another big waste
of platitudes and self-serving. The only reason I was
standing in the firing line was my class didn't start until
twelve-thirty, and I was sick to death of reading articles
about the history of the Miracle Play.

Maybe ten times he listened to my sketch of the noon
rally, where I'd been standing, how far from the nearest
dead student. "Fifty-three feet," he prompted each time.
"I went back and measured. There's enough landmarks
in your story; you don't forget things like that."

And then, while we were eating lunch, he told me
about the Nazi on the phone, how you could call the
white-power hot line and listen to somebody tell you the

revolution's here and it was time for people who qualified for the Aryan Nation to kick some tainted ass. "Listen to this," Dick said after he dragged me to a pay phone outside Arby's.

"America is weakened by the genetically inferior. The colored must be kept from the white. America is poisoned by the morally inferior. The heathen must be kept from the Christian," I heard, so I knew what would follow: "Black, brown, yellow, red must leave or perish. Jew, Muslim, non-believer must leave or perish," it went on, and then the tape ran out as if it were supposed to be a cliffhanger and maybe I'd call in next week for a fresh loop. The operator asked for thirty-five cents. I hung up like I hadn't heard her, and Dick waited for me to say something.

He was looking for shadows and darkness in my expression, and I didn't think I was giving him any. "Well?" he said.

I was puzzled, too. It was just a tape. It hadn't made me any more angry than a film villain who snuffs out a few extras' lives. "It's grotesque," I tried.

"That's it?" Dick said.

"Nobody takes this stuff seriously. It's like the promises that go with phone numbers on a men's room wall. Nobody calls those numbers."

"These guys are real. They originate from a place in Akron. There's a street number and everything. People know."

"In that case, we ought to go down and clean them out," I said, like a ten year-old.

Dick beamed. "That's talking. That's what I wanted to hear."

"They're the army, not us," I retreated.

"Why don't we call the Ohio Guard then? Why don't we call General Del Corso?"

"The house number's bogus. Nobody gives up a number like that."

"Why don't we call General Canterbury?"

"I've been close enough to foolishness for a while. I'm on R&R."

"Vacations end."

"They clear the head. They set you straight."

"That's the idea here."

"What's to see?" I said.

"Who knows? Some moron. Some redneck."

He wasn't going to find any Nazis, I thought. Nobody publicizing the virtues of white power would have any address but a post office box. Dick Dawson was always getting hot tips; he was a regular on the stairway to wealth. When summer school started, he dragged me down to the IGA Market because we were going to win five thousand dollars in their Cleveland Indians Lineup Game. All we had to do was complete the infield for the big money, the outfield for one hundred dollars; all we had to do was complete the battery for instant small cash,

We stole hundreds of game pieces, lifting them from the shelves beneath the registers of empty check-out lanes. "It's like five-years-worth of trips to the grocery store," Dick said. "It's like we've gone to the IGA every hour of every day since the contest began."

After we opened the first twenty game pieces, we already had Eddie Lion 2B, Greg Nettles 3B, and Jack Heidemann ss. In the outfield we had Ted Uhlaender

CF and Vada Pinson RF. Catching, we had Duke Sims. All we needed, with 300 pieces to go, was a first baseman or a left fielder or, if we didn't mind the small change, a pitcher.

"Come on, Tony Horton," Dick kept saying. "Come on, Hawk Harrelson." I was counting Eddie Leon cards. Pretty soon we had sixty of him, forty-five of Vada Pinson, forty of Duke Sims. "Come on," Dick was pleading, "give me Sam McDowell; give me that ten dollars ."

Duke Sims was gaining. He passed Vada Pinson and nearly overtook Eddie Leon. When we reached the last peel-off piece, there were sixty-eight pictures of him in his crouch, seventy-one of Leon crossing his body for a backhand stab. The last picture showed Ted Uhlaender shading his eyes from an imaginary sun. "It's fixed," Dick said. "Look at all these pictures of Sims, and he doesn't even start anymore. How come they don't have Fosse on these cards?"

"They guessed," I said. "They went with the status quo."

"When the hell did they print these things?"

"February," I said right away. I thought I was right; I thought the picture of Hawk Harrelson, if there was one in eastern Ohio, wouldn't show him with the leg he'd broken. The Hawk, while we were looking for his five thousand dollar face, was getting votes for the All-Star Game even though he was disabled, even though somebody named Roy Foster was trying to bat .250 and stay in the major leagues as the Indians first baseman.

*   *   *   *   *   *   *

Four hours later, after a lecture on the psychological

states of Wordsworth and Coleridge at each moment they wrote, after two more citizen witnesses, I followed Dick into his apartment. "Look at this kitchen," he said.

It had only been two days since I'd been in that kitchen, but I looked, wondering how large a damage deposit Dick put down when he signed the lease. The baseboards were gone, peeled from the walls. The tile was lifted and loose, as if it had been set back in place after a week of flood water worked it over. In one corner there were eight scattered blocks, and among those pieces of tile stood Dick Dawson's dog, a pure-white Samoyed. It looked from me to the tile and back again, growling, sizing up, probably, whether I was someone who ignored its kills in the past or someone who'd come about discipline.

"That dog's been busy," I said, remembering the baseboards in place two nights before.

"We decided to keep the damage to one site. We're sacrificing the kitchen instead of scattering ruin around the house."

"Your landlord approve that plan?"

"Samoyeds do this. You can't stop them except to fence them off from the things that matter." It looked to me as if Dick's dog could leap this gate if it wanted to start on the essential things. "Ok, Thor," Dick said, releasing the catch.

The dog bounded over and rushed through the open front door. In a minute it was back, but Dick didn't lock it in the kitchen again or slam it with his fist for destroying an entire room. "Thor won't hurt anything while we're here. It's not like he's gone crazy. It's only when he's left behind he eats things."

"Last time I was here it was only doing a little chewing, a little nip and tuck around the doorframes."

"Right," Dick said. "Here we were trying to keep him from marring everything in the apartment by giving him the kitchen to teethe on, a room with nothing we thought he could hurt. He must have been working on this place every minute we were gone yesterday. It's amazing what a dog can do when he sets his mind to it."

The Samoyed appeared satisfied. It wasn't cowering near any of the tooth-ridden walls. It was staring straight at both of us with the what-else-can-you-do-to-me glare of the death camp. "Live free or die," I said, but Dick didn't laugh.

"You're getting yourself one strange sense of humor," he said. "All your fear is getting misplaced."

I'd bought us two six-packs of Hop 'N Gator, a lemon-lime malt liquor Iron City was test marketing in western Pennsylvania and eastern Ohio. "Fag beer," Dick announced after taking his first swallow, and I had to admit it didn't taste like it could be delivering a malt liquor's worth of alcohol.

When she got home an hour later, Carol said she loved it, and Dick handed her one and searched out a Stroh's. Already the Hop 'N Gator wasn't sitting very well. It left an aftertaste that made me think of cyclamates. I thought maybe if you drank a dozen Hop 'N Gators every day for a year you deserved bladder cancer or whatever else the test mice acquired from diet soda. What I was accumulating, however, was an enormous headache, a cheap wine or bad gin sort of throbbing while Carol was drumming up dinner and the television was telling us about Angela Davis on the run after she supported one more anarchic tragedy in California.

I sat up when the newscast finished with a feature on somebody named Mrs. Pat Palinkas, who, it turned out, was the first woman to play in a professional football game. I'd never heard of the Orlando Panthers, but I was interested until the announcer admitted she was the holder for placekicks, that it was her husband doing the kicking. "You should have had Carol on one knee in the back yard," I said. "You should have kept practicing that sidewinder you picked up playing soccer."

Dick grunted. "Nothing about the hearings," he said. "We've dropped off the national news."

"We're in reruns," I said, and followed him back to the kitchen where Carol was about ready to feed us. She owned a thick, hardback cookbook with a green cover that said *McCall's*. Each night I'd eaten there she picked a salad, a meat, and a dessert recipe from its pages and sent them our way. She didn't seem to care whether or not the vegetables were in season, whether or not the foods complemented each other. This time it was porkchops in the middle of the table, sweet and sour probably, because they appeared to be dipped in rust-colored tar. They reminded me of how fossils might originate, stuck in glop for a billion years. And I knew, glancing at the page where she placed her bookmark, that I could look forward to Old-Fashioned Applesauce Cake, Favorite One-Egg Cake, or McCall's Best Gold Cake for dessert. *Now to find out how good a cook you really are*, it said on the first page of the Perfect Pies section. *The really good cook makes really good pie crusts.*

Thor circled the table throughout the meal. The Samoyed's nails clicked on what was left of the tile, and I wanted to tell it to sit by me so I could slip it all of my

Old-Fashioned Applesauce Cake. "Why do you put up with this dog?" I said.

"He's ours." Dick sounded like a father who'd just spent time talking to a police sergeant about his son and heard the words *Next time it'll go hard on the boy*.

"Hhaaah," Carol said at the end of her yawn.

I examined that kitchen again, saw how maybe that dog could worry the dry wall loose and then strip the panels right back to the wiring. "I know a guy back home who lost his dog," I said.

Carol stood up and walked to the refrigerator. She rummaged through the jars on a couple of shelves as if she couldn't finish her porkchop without something that hadn't been important when the meal began. "So how did he lose it?" Dick finally prompted.

"It barked at everything. It kept the guy up all night, so he tried putting it outside on a long leash, and it would fly off the porch and lunge at cars or whoever happened by on the sidewalk. It turned out, though, the leash was long enough for the dog to reach his bedroom window, and now it kept him up all night snuffling and growling."

I paused to see if Carol was finished. She was standing in front of the open refrigerator as if its light were an evil eye. "The dog hung itself," she said to the shelves, and Dick raised his eyebrows at me. I gave her a few seconds to complete the story for me, but she didn't turn around.

"Well, the guy shortened its leash," I started back in. "He decided he couldn't have the dog breathing under his window every night, and then the dog flew off the porch the next evening and didn't quite touch down. Snapped its neck. He found it dangling there in the morning after the best night's sleep he'd had in months."

"Maybe one of the neighbors tossed it off the porch," Dick suggested.

"Could be."

"Hhaaah," Carol exhaled, coming back to the table at last. She added, "Maybe that fellow measured that leash to get things exactly right."

* * * * * * *

After the applesauce cake, Dick and I ended up standing near the edge of the grass lot he shared with the other tenant in the double. The Hop 'N Gator, by then, had given me something that seemed like what I'd feel when the aneurysm of the year 2000 struck me down, my version of the millenium of every religion that promised an ending both concrete and dated.

"Look at all the fireflies," Dick said, and I had to agree. There were thousands. They blinked on and off as if excited to be out there in the middle of August, as if they didn't know it was just about the witching hour for fireflies in that part of the country. I waved at every one of them, trying to think of the collective noun for fireflies—a host, a swarm, a throng—but I heard Dick say, "You're thinking the frontal attack plan is stupid, right?"

I didn't have to answer. "I'll tell you how stupid I think it is," Dick said. "I'm going to drive right into Akron with or without you. I'm going to Light-Brigade the Nazis with or without any plan."

I looked at the flat Ohio countryside. Nothing I saw appeared threatening or evil. The landscape was monotonous. I didn't want to live here, but I didn't imagine people or objects inherently awful. I turned to Dick and said, "That guy today, the Nazi on the phone, he said 'So dare to be great.'"

"Sounds like somebody raised on Dr. Spock," Dick said. "Like somebody who failed everything he was allowed to try and then was too dumb to grow up."

I nodded, but Dick was drumming on his bottle and staring at the yard as if it were pocked with sinkholes. I felt alone, left behind to chew on what he'd already discarded. I felt like Thor in the afternoons, like I was staring out over the locked gate of the future thinking, *Well, that's it. Nobody's coming back.*

The fireflies seemed to be disappearing, as if a sort of low-lying cloud cover had moved in. The yard split where the light from inside cut it; the door slammed and the lawn was whole again. Thor bounded between us, choosing to leap against Dick's thigh before it nosed along the back fence for the perfect place to take a leak. If I had been staying with any other couple, Carol would have followed the dog outside and brought a beer. Or Dick would have called for her to join us.

* * * * * * *

The next morning I walked to campus from Dick's apartment. I was feeling shaky from the unknowns in the Hop 'N Gator and imagined the mile would do me good before class. Halfway, things hadn't improved, so I stopped and had coffee and a doughnut and the morning paper.

Mayor Satrom speaks today, it said on the front page. *The real story of the trashing of downtown Kent gets its day in court.* I turned the page. I knew what Mayor Satrom had to say, so I followed a column's worth of quotes from Melvin Laird, read his assurances that the nerve gas the army dumped into the ocean off Florida two days before wouldn't hurt anything because it was 16,000 feet deep. *Regardless*, the Secretary of Defense explained, *such a dumping will never happen again.*

Sure, I thought, paging to the Want Ads, checking to see if the Nazis had placed a recruiting notice. The columns looked as benign as the restaurant menu; I was as fueled as I could stand, left a dollar on the table, and started to do what I could about completing my pre-Shakespeare requirement. In two hours I'd meet Dick Dawson at the hearings. I didn't want him to do all the translating, adding his interpretation to the Rashomon of August.

A woman and a teenage girl approached. From a half block away there was no question the girl was the woman's daughter, but suddenly the woman steered the girl left, guided her off the curb and across the street to the other side. Although she was probably fifteen, the girl didn't resist. She acted like she was on a Trust Walk, like she was willingly blind to demonstrate there was at least one person in the world she would follow without question. She stared at me from across the street, and I thought the Hop 'N Gator had turned me green. "It's your hair, fella," I heard from behind me.

I pivoted. The man who spoke wore jeans and a sleeveless t-shirt. His hair was slicked back and smooth. Valentino, I thought. My father twenty years ago. "And that dipsy-doo mustache. You look like somebody oughta got hisself plugged a while back."

"Thanks for the insight," I said, but the man kept on.

"You look like you been whupped with the shit stick, fella. You look like you caught the short end."

I'd never heard of the shit stick, but I was getting his drift. The woman's daughter was still staring from the opposite sidewalk. I thought it was the kind of look you might receive from the last passenger to cram into the lifeboat as it was rowing away from where you were bent over the railing of a fire-swept ocean liner.

Somebody like her mother had testified the week before. She said she was afraid to walk the streets of Kent because she didn't know what the students might do. I hadn't blamed her. I didn't know what I could do either. I'd been there when those fifty-four rounds were fired, but if they called me to the stand, they'd have at least one witness who wouldn't testify he was sure of himself, unlike Del Corso and Canterbury and the briarhopper looking at me with his I-want-to-kick-your-ass face on because my hair was two inches over my collar.

And when I found Dick after the morning hearings were over, saw him working his way back from the front rows where he must have sat for an hour before Satrom started in with *The disturbances were planned*, I said "I've been giving some thought to Akron."

Dick brightened. "Malice and mayhem," he said.

"Maybe," I said. "I've been thinking, that's all. We have a round of golf to play."

"You're screwing with me."

"We have plenty of time. Nine holes is two hours. I'll give you yes or no when we're done."

"The therapy of the leisure class," Dick said.

"If you say so."

"Getting things straight."

The first hole on the university course, a par four, was only 305 yards, and every time I teed off I imagined a hole in one, a couple of bounces on the fairway, the roll onto the green and down. Somebody would do it, but it wasn't going to be me after I rotated early and over-swung, hooking the ball so I had to search for it in the deep rough while a foursome stood watching as if they were thinking of teeing off and maybe matching my shot yard for yard with right to left spin.

I laid up short. I chipped to the back of the green and three-putted while Dick dropped a six-footer for par. And then, on the next hole, I let go a banana hook that drifted off the course entirely. "Nobody hooks like that," Dick said. "Those cows don't see golf balls, not on a short par three."

"What the hell," I tried. "There's no out of bounds." I figured I was sixty yards left on a 140 yard hole. From outside the fence, the cows seemed stupidly passive, background for all the boring two-lane highways I'd been driving in the eight years I'd had a license. As soon as I stepped into the field, though, they raised their heads and pawed the earth. I knew dairy cattle weren't supposed to be aggressive, but my ball lay less than twenty feet from a cow eyeing me like I was something that would feel good under its hooves.

I worked my way into position. I used all the excuses of the unusual recovery to account for pivoting slowly, addressing the ball as if it were plugged in sand. And when I heard the cow shuffle, I imagined it striking me from behind, a cow's version of the grade school behind-the-knees trick, and kicking at my face when I fell.

Despite whatever good sense I had, I stepped back and turned to look. The cow was maybe a step closer, but it wasn't moving. "Watch out for Elsie," Dick said. He was leaning on his bag by the green.

There was nothing to do but step up and slap the ball quickly, a line drive that rolled through the green and stopped in the fringe on the opposite side. Not bad, really, I thought. The cow began strolling toward me, and I turned my back to hurry toward the fence like all the idiots in failed-escape stories.

"They're killers, you know," Dick said as I approached the green. "They take advantage of people who think they're stupid."

"Sure," I said. I'd visited a dozen farms. I'd ridden horses. There was nothing frightening about a field of cows.

"Borden's revenge," Dick said.

I used the putter from the apron and guessed the speed so lucky the ball died a foot from the hole. "Good up, Tex."

I tapped in. I wanted to tell Dick about the difference between walking through a field and hitting a golf ball from it. "I'm rolling now," I said. "I'll play you even up for the trip to Akron. You win, we go; I win, we drink beer like sane people."

Dick made par and smiled. "You giving me the three strokes I already have?"

"Sure."

"Ok, cowboy."

Behind us I heard one of the cows make a sound that, had I not known what was in that field, I would have called a growl. An hour later I'd made up the strokes, was plus one as we teed off on number nine. With maybe 120 yards to the flag, though, I flopped my approach under the lip of a trap, barely escaped, and three-putted from fifty feet to lose by one. "Here we go," Dick said.

"I guess."

"They're not cows," Dick said.

"That's right."

"They're not going to stampede."

"Sure."

* * * * * * *

It turned out we had to walk fifteen blocks, crossing and recrossing South Arlington Street, because Dick admitted, once we parked on Market, he only knew the Nazis were "on Arlington between the expressways." It was two miles of hunt and peck in a neighborhood where you save up for a down payment so you can move away. Planes skimmed overhead as they approached, I hoped, at the right altitude for the runways a half mile away. And though I knew better, I thought maybe it was the air quality from the Firestone and Goodyear plants making me sick of the afternoon.

We'd covered about a mile and a half, closing in on Route 224, when Dick said "There." I looked where he was pointing and saw a door which said *So. Arlington Services*. Whatever Dick knew, that door wasn't giving it away.

I followed him inside before I had a chance to tell him this looked like a long shot. There was a tiny foyer and a flight of stairs leading to Christ knew what. The walls were black with a few white graffiti etchings somebody probably carved after pissing in the stairwell. I searched for *Kill Kent State Students*, but there was only stuff like *I give good head/426-3472* and, underneath it, *Fags eat shit*.

It reminded me of the stairs I had to climb to reach the dentist on Pittsburgh's North Side. *Dr. Mendel/Dr. Murray* it said on a door at the top of those stairs, but you had to trust those names to be there each time you returned six months later for another checkup. The door across the hall said *Allegheny Talent Associates. Who went in there?* I wondered for ten years. For all I knew, *Allegheny Talent Associates* was auditioning tap dancers, ventriloquists, and accordion players while I was accumulating fillings, was auditioning, even now, another generation of vaudevillians.

"Here we go," Dick said.

"Sure we do."

"What's the worst that can be up there?"

I thought there'd be nothing at all up there but abandoned offices, that Dick had gotten some ludicrous directions because nobody would expect anyone to follow up on a tip like *Upstairs at So. Arlington Associates.* I shrugged and said, "Crazies in boots. Shaved heads and machine guns."

"White power groupies."

"Right."

"Hitler's finest."

I figured Dick, by now, understood there was nothing upstairs but emptiness, because there we went, right to the dead-end landing that offered us the three doors of a thousand fables. All of them had smoked-glass windows. One said *Rubber City Enterprises*; one said *Akron Planning Systems*; one, improbably, claimed it opened to an *M.D.*

"Let's try Dr. Siejka," I said. "Maybe it's Rumanian for mass murderer."

"That's thinking," Dick answered, turning the knob on *Rubber City Enterprises* before I could tell him I'd changed my mind about this trip.

It was locked. I twisted Siejka's doorknob to make sure he was out for the day as well, and then there was only one more chance we'd get slaughtered by idiots waiting for the second coming.

Dick pushed on the door to *Akron Planning Systems*, and it opened so easily I thought for a moment normal people might be inside writing government proposals to renovate South Arlington Street.

"Can I help you?" a woman asked Dick from behind a solid-looking wooden desk.

"We've erred," I said to Dick.

"Is this where the call-line originates?" he asked her.

"Pardon me?"

"The recorded messages."

"I'm sorry."

"Dial-A-Hate. Gestapo hit parade."

"Do you have an appointment?"

"I want an interview."

The door behind her opened. The man who stood in the doorway was dressed to sell insurance. "What can we do for you?" he said.

"Is this the Nazi hotline headquarters?"

"I'm afraid you're mistaken."

"What if I said we wanted to join? A haircut and brain damage would turn us into brown shirts."

The door at the bottom of the steps slammed. Five minutes ago I hadn't been able to imagine one person ever entering this building, and now we had a traffic jam. I was waiting for Dick to look like he heard it, too, something that would jog him into common sense. "I guess I'll pass on the trim," he said then, so I knew he'd picked up on the two sets of footsteps on the stairs, could subtract the locked doors from the chances they were headed elsewhere.

"I understand," the man in the doorway said. "Where do you think you are, friend?"

Dick said "I'm right here," but he'd already let himself glance back at the outer door.

The two men who entered wore long-sleeved white shirts and dark ties, as if dressed to witness for the Mormon Church. They seemed harmless. Like the students who handed out leaflets in the snack bar, but neither of them greeted us with a sunny phrase. "And who might you be, friend?" the insurance agent asked.

"Come on," I said to Dick as if we had a choice.

"You need a map, friend. It's a sunny day; it's very dark on the stairs. Perhaps you've made a mistake," and both of us kept quiet, acting like we were at gunpoint or had been caught plagiarizing our junior high school social studies project.

The stairway was as dark as the manager of *Akron Planning Systems* described. We walked down in a world that had turned to sound and touch: the shoe on wood, the hand on wallboard, the back of our heads sending sonar up the stairs behind us to sweep for echoes of clubs or knives or guns. When we reached the sidewalk, we treaded water for maybe ten seconds until Dick said "See?"

I stood where somebody impatient with my tainted blood could have shot me from the stairwell. Enough of my brain activated to force *Walk* to my feet. If Dick wanted to know what I'd seen, he'd have to keep up.

"Right out in the open," he said, matching my cadence.

"I guess."

"That means the cops let them. That means they have support."

The real street returned then. I listened to each building we passed and heard nothing but the white noise of traffic. We headed south, adding another block to our return trip, but crossed the street before we started back toward the car. Across from the *So. Arlington Associates* front door, Dick stopped again, and I had to wait for him to make a gesture.

Whatever he was going to say, I would have to disagree. I knew that as soon as he started clenching and unclenching his fists. He said, "We have an obligation here. We have to do our part for civilization," so disagreeing wasn't hard.

It was as easy to smirk at as the *McCall's* recipes that relied on adjectives. Puffy. Crispy. Perfect. A month before, when I read the Justice Department's memo after it was released by the *Akron Beacon Journal,* I'd been smug for days. "I shot two teenagers," a guardsman had been quoted, and I wanted a little frontier justice of my own. Listening to Dick's certainties, however, I understood I was lost.

"So what are our choices?" he pushed.

I wanted to get us moving north, guide us toward the punctuation of yawns and another savory dinner. "What does that mean?" I said.

"Our choices. We have to do something now we know they're really here."

"They'll move on. They won't stay in one office more than a month or two."

"They want to be found. They want confrontation."

"And we're required to provide it?"

"Yes."

"By some force."

"Something like that."

"By decency."

"Yes."

I wanted to say, "Hhaaah." I wanted to talk Thor into spending the night in the *Akron Planning Systems* office. "And if we don't do anything?" I said.

"That's not in question here. Do you think it's in question?"

"Sure it's in question."

"So," Dick said, and he unraveled his fists. "You haven't been moved."

"I didn't say that."

"That's what I'm hearing."

I began to walk north. I knew Dick could recruit a commando squad and leave me out. I thought about the simplicity of action, that I was willing to walk all the way back to Kent, where the improbable volley had suddenly been fired, that I could stand being left behind by Dick, that I could watch him set out alone to invade the lair of the goon squad.

So I stayed shut up when I reached his car and turned to see him closing the distance between us. And I stayed shut up as he pulled onto Eastland Avenue for the drive through Tallmadge, out Route 261 into Kent. I didn't care what he had to say about the Nazis. I thought they had as much chance at success as a couple of hundred protesting students. For all I knew, the Akron Nazis had four members, as far on the fringe as some loonies making bombs in a basement to free white rats and hamsters from a laboratory.

"You're thinking all of this is stupid, right?" Dick said at last.

I didn't have to answer. A few seconds of silence was all Dick could listen to before he'd start in again. "I'll tell you how stupid I think it is," he said. "I feel like turning around right now and laying some waste to that office. I feel like dropping you off halfway through my U-turn."

"Whatever," I said, although I agreed with him there was something wrong with somebody like me who couldn't find intensity in things. And as soon as I thought it, I didn't believe it was a terrible thing at all.

For Keepsies

"Baker, baker!"

Crumley was listening just like I was, but I didn't have to do anything because it was Crumley who was being paged.

"Baker, baker!"

I wanted to say something like "Let's drag the dumb jerk inside before he freezes," but I was afraid of Crumley's silence, how he judged everything without talking. "I got the rolls made up," I said. "You want 'em in the oven?"

"Give 'em a minute," Crumley said. Otis Redding was on the radio, but it was turned down low from the first time we'd heard the drunk shouting from outside in the snow. "She may be weary," Otis started, "and young girls they do get weary . . ."

"Baker, baker!" the drunk shouted again, sounding as if he were yelling through a crack in the foundation, and Crumley snapped Otis Redding off. For a second I had the first pan of rolls up and ready to flip over in a rage, but that would've been too stupid, even for a nowhere nineteen-year-old like me, waiting around for a draft notice while doing baker's help.

I slid the pan into the oven where I'd taken out a rack of bread. I started back for a second pan and Crumley shoved by me for the door. "Dumb ass'll die out there," he said, "and then what'll we have."

Crumley had the drunk inside before I'd finished with the rolls. "Dead weight," he said, dragging the body to a chair by the space heater near one of the display cases. The drunk looked to be about forty-five, maybe fifty, Crumley's age; he had vomit stuck on one side of his face, so I didn't want to look at him too long.

"Nobody cleans him up," Crumley said.

"No problem."

"We keep him alive, but we don't have to be nurse-maids."

I wasn't arguing, but I wasn't sure whether or not we were keeping him alive. He slumped back by the space heater with his mouth open, and it sounded like he was gargling salt water for a sore throat, like his throat was full of snot or he'd inhaled some vomit.

"Bob Case," Crumley said. "You get to know every-body in a place like this." I stood around waiting for him to get it over with. "This guy used to play third base for Miller's. You believe that? Bob Case." Crumley sat him up a little, unbuttoned his coat. "Soft, quick hands. You gotta have quick hands at third and now look at him."

"Yeah," I said.

Crumley snorted. "Yeah," he said. "Yeah is right."

We went back to work. The rolls got themselves ready, and Crumley had me haul them to the storefront. The drunk was still there. He had his mouth closed now, so he'd been doing something while the rolls baked, and I stood behind the counter waiting for him to look up and notice me.

I wanted to hear what he had to say about pitching into the snow at three A.M. and forgetting how to get up, but he didn't look like he was ready to tell stories. I went back for another pan of rolls, then another, and waited again, watching the drunk named Bob Case get all he could out of that space heater. His face, because his body was hunched over so far, was maybe six inches from the surface. When he finally glanced up at me it was as if he'd had enough of inhaling something from the coils.

"Hell of a night," he said. He probably expected me to agree with him, get something in common going between us, so I started arranging rolls in the wall-length case. "Hard to tell from in here," I said.

"Hell of a place to work," he said. "All this stuff's gotta get to you. Like being a goddamned bartender or something."

"You want a roll?" I tried. I held out a bear claw, figuring Crumley wouldn't mind, but Bob Case wasn't ready for walking over to take it, so I left it on the counter top. "For later," I said. "For walking home with."

"I tried that already," he said. "It didn't work out."

"Take your time. You'll get your legs back."

I heard Crumley opening and closing the ovens. He probably had something for me to get to, something he'd be doing already when I got back so I'd see how easily he could get along without me.

"What the fuck do you know?" Bob Case said. "What the fuck do you know about any goddamned thing?"

"It's Ok," I said, listening to Crumley, trying to tell if he was listening to me. "It's just a bad night."

"What the fuck do you know about bad nights? What the fuck kind of bad night you ever had puking up your daddy's beer?"

I didn't have any more rolls to put away. I didn't want to leave as if an old fool like Bob Case with vomit stuck to the side of his face could scare me off, so I said "Dumb asshole" and got ready for whatever he was out of control enough to do.

"But this dumb asshole ain't doin' no woman's work," he said. His face dropped again and I thought he was through, but then he added, "I know Frank Crumley, and you see how long he left me lay out there freezing."

I didn't have anything to offer about Crumley and his judgment, so I backed through the door and left Bob Case to doze off if he wanted. "You see?" Crumley said. He was pounding a mound of dough, slapping the yeast-driven bubble back into a bottom-of-the-bowl glob. I pushed a rack of pans over to the workbench knowing Crumley wasn't through: "Do the world a favor if I'd left him out there. One less burned-out bum who thinks he's earned his binges." Crumley saw me glance at the radio. "Go ahead," he said, "turn it back on. I'm tired of the Good Samaritan Hour."

The Temptations were singing "Ain't Too Proud to Beg."

"Don't white people sing anymore?" Crumley said.

"What the fuck do I know?" I said, and Crumley laughed.

"Yeah, right," he said. He listened to a couple of lines. "You see what happened in South Africa, don't you?"

I looked up South Africa in my brain and didn't find many entries. "The heart transplant?" I said.

"See?" Crumley said. "You know all about it?"

There wasn't anything in South Africa I knew all about, so I had to say "I don't follow."

"The Blacks." I put on my best empty-head expression. Crumley nodded at the radio. "The niggers," he said, "they're gettin' into everything." I kept the look on for another few seconds. "That guy Washansky, whatever his name is," Crumley said, "they gave him a nigger heart; they gave him nigger blood."

"He's alive."

"Damn right he's alive, and he's just the first one. They marry whites and now they get inside us, too, with their hearts and their kidneys and their livers and whatever else you can exchange."

"It's not an exchange," I said, and Crumley stared right past me at the radio. "The donor doesn't get anything in return."

"The hell he doesn't," Crumley said.

"I don't know."

"Yeah," Crumley said, "Bob Case is dead drunk and sees that."

A group called the Lemonpipers came on singing "Green Tambourine." "Listen," I said, "these guys are white; they're even in college somewhere."

"I'll bet you something," Crumley said. "I'll bet you that roll walks out of here with Bob Case."

*   *   *   *   *   *   *   *

"Otis Redding's dead," Jack said. SueAnne and Carol were giggling in the booth Jack's father had built into the corner of the basement. It made the room look like a diner, the bar we were sitting at running half the length of it. Those girls laughing made me want to go over and slap both of them. "You hear me?" Jack said.

"Otis Redding's dead," I said.

"His plane crashed into Lake Erie or someplace."

"Or someplace," I said. I felt like I was in church. I felt like I was supposed to be saying my lines with intensity, and I just kept thinking about slapping the girls until they got quiet, maybe bruising their faces so they'd remember who I was.

"He's the man," Jack said, "and now he's gone. Some goddamned stupid plane crash like Buddy Holly's."

I kept the can at my mouth until the Iron City was gone. "Shit," I said, "when'd it happen?"

"Last night. Goddamned Cleveland. Goddamned shitty-assed place to fly out of in December."

"He's been dead a day and nobody knew?"

"They knew. We just didn't hear about it."

"You heard about it. You're telling me."

"I saw it in the paper upstairs when I went up to take a piss."

"Respect is what I want, respect is what I need," I started, but then it sounded dumb, so I just said, "Where'd he end up?"

"At the bottom of the goddamned lake."

"No. In the paper. Second page? Third page?"

"First page," Jack said, "Or I wouldn't have noticed just walking by."

"Top or bottom?"

"Bottom."

"See?"

The girls laughed again. They'd been talking all night about Lynda Bird Johnson's wedding, how they'd settle for one tenth of what she'd had. "Which tenth?" I'd said a half an hour ago, but they hadn't gotten what I meant and I didn't have enough beer in me yet to press it. Now they were at the silly stage of getting drunk, tiresome the second time you see it, the way child actors get on a TV series, working with a laugh track so they never change until they're canceled or start getting pimples.

I turned my back to the girls, asked Jack for a shot of his father's Imperial. "For Otis," I said, and he poured himself one, chasing it with his Iron so we could start paying attention to our drinking.

"For Buddy Holly," Jack said, pouring another one. The girls ran out of funny things to tell each other about White House weddings and came over for a refill. Jack filled shot glasses for them. He didn't offer any Squirt or Seven-Up.

"For Richie Valens," I said and nodded at the shot glasses.

"Why not?" Carol tried. She tilted her head way back so she wouldn't stop the whiskey.

SueAnne looked at her drink. "For J. P. Richardson," I said. She didn't say anything, but she swallowed the shot.

"Did we pass?" Carol said. "Did we earn something?"

"For Patsy Cline," I said. "For Jim Reeves."

"You're shut off," Jack said, and we both laughed so the girls would feel left out of what we were sharing.

"Probably while drunk old Bob Case was nodding off in the bakery," I started. "Probably Crumley was dragging in the old jerk from the alley right when Otis was falling out of the sky."

"You guys are out of it," SueAnne said. "You know that?"

"Otis is out of it," I said. "That's who's out of it."

A week later Crumley got a letter from his father who was living in one of those condominium developments that were filling up all the usable land in Florida. "I got a letter from Fort Lauderdale, I know I've got trouble," Crumley said.

I was greasing bread pans; my shift was only fifteen minutes old, so I knew anything Crumley talked about this early must be bothering him. "He's got spots," Crumley started, and I slapped the brush around the inside of the pans, something like varnishing wood. "On his lungs, you know, both of them, so there's nothing they can do."

"They've got ways," I said, but I didn't know any off-hand.

"You get cancer in one lung, they take it out; you get cancer in two lungs, they bury you." I tried to hurry a little, wanted to make sure Crumley wouldn't use me to punish for his father's dying.

"It's all the stuff in the air," he kept on. "You'll see. Everything's falling apart earlier and earlier. What chance do lungs have if bridges start collapsing because the stuff in the air eats them up?" He was watching me, I thought, timing me by the pan maybe and waiting for me to argue. I had the brush to keep me out of trouble.

"They're not saying anything, but that bridge down the river was all eaten away. The Silver Bridge? The silver part just covered up the problem so all those Christmas shoppers could drop right into the goddamned Ohio."

"How many people died?" I said. "They find out yet?"

"Thirty-six," Crumley said right away, "but they're still looking. Goddamned bridge collapsing. You never heard of that when I was a kid because all that stuff wasn't in the air."

I thought of the guy who'd been interviewed on TV, the guy who'd been in the first car not to have plunged into the river; I thought of Crumley's father standing on one of those little balconies they give you so you can look out at the ocean and feel lucky to be in Florida in December. "I don't know," I said.

"Let me tell you something about my father," Crumley said. "He worked on bridges. He helped build the Liberty Bridge, the one that goes into the Tubes so you can get the hell out of Pittsburgh if you live in the South Hills."

Crumley had never said anything about his father except that he lived in Florida. I had another ten minutes worth of pans, so all I had to do was listen: "I was just a kid when it got finished. 1928. My father took me to the opening, and the whole bridge was nothing but cars. Like a parking lot. Bumper to bumper, and it didn't fall. It didn't fall in 1936 either when it looked like the whole city was dead in the water. St. Patrick's Day flood, you've heard of it?"

"Yeah."

"Nothing like it since. Nothing like that Liberty Bridge my father built still standing under all those rush hours. Now we got bridges collapsing. Now we got bridges just sitting there half-done and never getting finished. Goddamned goldbricks. Goddamned welfare."

I knew the half-done bridge first hand—Pittsburgh's "Bridge to Nowhere." There were bumper stickers; there were protests and still it hung out over the Monongahela half-done and nobody working on it for over a year. I pulled down the last batch of bread pans. "Got these done in a minute," I said.

"Goddamned cancer," Crumley said. "Nobody got cancer when I was a kid either." He put his hands on the pan rack and leaned toward me. "You know that? Nobody got cancer then because there wasn't all this artificial stuff in the air."

"It was pretty smoky, wasn't it?" I tried.

"Goddamned right it was smoky. It was smoky as hell." I put the last pan on the rack and Crumley backed it up and turned to push it. "But it was real smoke. It was real stuff burning, not this pretend stuff that eats up peoples' lungs until they drown just like the poor bastards who got dumped with the Silver Bridge."

*   *   *   *   *   *   *   *

I had never had a Christmas anywhere but in my living room. SueAnne's parents acted like they'd never had anybody but SueAnne and her sister to celebrate with, so everybody got miserable in a hurry.

During dinner her father asked me if I was ready for Vietnam. "You all in one piece?" he asked. "You 1-A and no excuses?"

"Dad," SueAnne said.

"This is important," her father said, but I didn't answer right away. I was 1-A and hoping the whole thing would blow over before my notice came. Instead, I said "No excuses" after I'd pretended to finish chewing turkey.

"Breaks my heart to see America make excuses," he

said. "We're like snot-nosed kids taking notes from Mommy to the teacher."

He poured all of us a second glass of wine. I noticed it was the same kind I'd had once or twice while driving around on a Saturday, the kind with a screw-off cap, like on a bottle of tomato juice.

The wine didn't change things. Everybody stayed quiet, cleaning up gravy and stuffing, but just before the pumpkin pie, SueAnne's father poured a third round for himself and me.

He started in one last time. "Look," he said, "we can't afford to let any slant-eyed country push us around. Next thing you know it'll give The Bear ideas."

"Maybe," I said.

"America doesn't lose wars."

"I guess not."

"Name one war we ever lost."

"I don't know. How about Korea?"

"Korea doesn't count. We didn't lose Korea. We won Korea and then we gave it back."

"I don't know. I thought I heard about it somewhere."

"Like some damn little snot-nosed kids on a playground."

"Like funsies," I said. SueAnne looked over at me, worrying. I thought maybe the wine was working.

"Yeah, like funsies," her father said. "You've played those games, too; for funsies, for keepsies."

Stored some place at my mother's was a big box full of baseball cards I'd won for keepsies, skimming them against the grade school wall. I let him pour me another glass.

"For keepsies," he said. "For one goddamned time for keepsies."

We had to go. I was taking SueAnne into Pittsburgh to the Syria Mosque for something called the Christmas Shower of Stars—thirteen acts, two songs each except for the headliners who did half an hour each. Tonight it was Little Anthony and the Imperials, Joe Tex right before them; there was even a white group, The Shangrilas, to maybe mix the crowd, which is what SueAnne was hoping.

"You drive careful now," her father said. "You get yourself back here in one piece."

"It's Ok," I said.

"It's getting my daughter back here in one piece with her slid over into the death seat."

Sue pushed her lips together. "I know," her father said, "Shut up, Dad, but you can't tell me you'll be hugging any doors."

*   *   *   *   *   *   *   *

"It's going to hell over there," Crumley said after the holidays. We were back on a regular schedule; we were finishing up sandwich buns, rolling them into balls in the hollows of our palms.

"Looks that way," I said.

"It more than looks that way. It is."

I was slowing us down again because I couldn't get my left hand to make circles. Everything on the left side of me seemed to be damaged. Practice making these buns hadn't helped, not six months of it. Crumley spun out sandwich buns with both hands, doubling me and not seeming to mind. "You'll kick some ass when you get there. It'll get done before your tour's up. Johnson's unloading on those gooks."

"Maybe," I said, though as soon as I said it, I knew I wasn't going to make any difference. I couldn't even roll two sandwich buns at once.

We racked the buns, giving them a chance to raise. "One game of HORSE," Crumley said, and I got the wadded up bread bag from beside the radio. Gary Puckett and the Union Gap was on, but they were as boring as ever, nothing I was going to miss playing HORSE.

We had a number 10 can nailed on the wall in the oven room where the ceiling stood a couple of feet higher. Two or three times a night we shot around, but it was tough to pop anything long because you'd hit ceiling anyway. I didn't care. I could jam on the nine-foot hoop. Better yet, Crumley relaxed and stopped grading everything for a few minutes.

We stuck a couple of easy ones to get started, six footers straight on, and then we tried hook shots and swishers until Crumley put it behind his back and over his head, missing his prayers often enough that pretty soon I only had HO and he was strung out on HORS.

Crumley always wasted too many turns on shots that went in maybe once a week, too many high risks that would stick me with a quick letter if he made one, but would never spell me out before I'd have him on the brink. Now, though, with four letters and the chance to choose shots, he moved inside and said, "Left hand, bank," kissing it off the wall and in.

I wasn't close, banking it up so high I didn't even catch rim. "You better not break that right hand of yours," Crumley said. "You won't even be able to jack off." He moved back a step and said, "Left hand, swish," but the paper ball kicked off the rim before it dropped through.

"You're the one going to need a transplant," I said, and I popped in a jumper from ten feet, a tough one because you couldn't get the right arc from that far out. "That'll get you E," I said.

"Hell it will." Crumley fired a flat one and lucked it in on a pinball shot. "Hey," he said, "you see that?"

"Yeah," I said, picking up the paper wad, surprised he was staying so interested, knowing, suddenly, that Crumley was going to play percentages and sit on the left hand bank until I was dead if I didn't spell him out of there while I was calling the shots.

I stepped back to around twelve feet, concentrating. "That Washansky guy didn't work out, did he. Maybe they should've given him a heart from his own kind." I sighted on the front rim, but Crumley kept at it. "You gotta check on things like that when you get transfusions. It's in the blood just like it's in the air." Finally, I just let it fly and dropped another one.

"E," I said. "E for sure."

"Washansky is for sure," said Crumley, and then he shut up and paid attention like you would if you thought somebody was holding the phone, waiting to call the score into the newspapers. He hit the back rim and the bread bag spun off to the side.

"Farewell shot," I said, but nobody made those, past fifteen feet with no arc at all.

He shook his head. "Maybe it'll happen," I tried, tossing him the bag. He shrugged and stepped back as far as he could.

"It's nothing but a miracle shit-shot," he said. "Who would ever think up something as dumb as this?" He fired his bullet and it smacked against the front of the can. "Back to work," he said. "Doughnuts."

I jammed one and caught it with my left hand before it hit the ground, but Crumley wasn't looking. Doughnuts weren't so bad. When they were done, my night was over. It was just Crumley on his own finishing up cream puffs and cake decorating.

As soon as I walked in the door, Jack said, "You see this shit on the news?"

He was so worked up I thought maybe James Brown might be dead, maybe a whole concert tour worth of soul singers blown up in some blizzard in Nebraska. "What's up?" I said.

"The Commies. They're blowing the shit out of everything."

"Give me some slack."

"They're everywhere, I swear to God. They're fucking us over right and left."

I flipped the channel to another network where a map of Vietnam was superimposed beside the announcer. Two forks of arrows were spreading across the map, and both of them were pointed south. "The offensive coincides with Tet," the announcer said, "the Vietnamese New Year."

"New Year's is over," Jack said.

"No, it isn't."

"Damn Commies even change New Year's."

I listened to what the announcer was saying. I looked at that map and started learning the names of places I was going to be before 1968 was over. "We're gone," I said. "We're on the bus by spring."

"We'll kick ass."

"Sure we will."

"We'll kick ass and get drunk for a month."

"Sure."

"Fucking Commies. Fucking Chinks."

"Gooks."

"Huh?"

"These Commies are Gooks; the Chinese Commies are Chinks."

"You an expert already?"

"We got the girls to pick up," I said. "We got a party to start."

"All over town," said Jack.

We tried. We got underage into six different bars, three of them with live bands, but all night I kept thinking that Crumley had been right somehow, that things were falling apart because of stuff in the air, that Otis Redding had probably flown through such a cloud of stuff that the plane had given out and plummeted right into Wisconsin.

By the time we'd had enough, there was nothing left to do but ride around Pittsburgh showing off Jack's Corvette. We still had a six pack we'd picked up before we left the last bar, so we opened our cans and jammed into the Corvette. SueAnne relaxed on my lap, and it felt good having her settle back against me, Carol pressing against me, too, because she was giving Jack more room than usual after he ran the first stoplight.

"Goddamned Commies," he said.

"Give it a rest," Carol tried. "Slow down a little."

"Vietnam," he said. "I don't even know how to pronounce it. 'RAM' or 'BOMB'—which is it?"

"RAM," I said, but I didn't have any idea.

"You sure?"

"What's the difference?" SueAnne said. She was lying back against me; my free hand had found her breasts under her coat.

"You need to know how to say things right. You don't want to sound like a foreigner."

We ran a second light, clipping along at eighty beside the river, but I was thinking about the way SueAnne was letting me keep my hand on her, how I might even unbutton her sweater because worrying about anybody else looking at us didn't matter anymore.

"Slow down, Jack," Carol said again.

"That new bridge is down here someplace," he said. "That damn bridge they never finished for a year now. That one the city won't pay for, the one the state won't pay for."

"Somebody went off it in a car," I said, adding, as if it were news, "and he lived." I was thinking about the way the interviewed survivor of the Silver Bridge disaster had said he'd gotten out of his car and looked down at the water, shivering, not even caring whether the section he was standing on might drop into the Ohio with him still on it. "He landed in the mud and walked."

"Right here," Jack said, and swerved hard right, skidding, my window turning yellow with road-crew machinery rushing at my eyes, blinking dark again as Jack retrieved the slide and turned us into the first barricade, one of those jumbo-sized wooden horses that the Corvette carried sideways into the second, like the start of a *Guiness Record Book* domino ripple, tumbling a third and opening up a slot to the brink where we would have been launched except the car dug in and rocked to a stop where my view was so much empty space.

Carol was screaming then as if her voice had just caught up with us. She kept at it, making up for the silence the rest of us were in. Jack was saying "Shit," over and over, pounding on the wheel like someone warming up to work over a face. And the beer was all over us. It was still dripping from the bottle I'd dropped into SueAnne's lap. She didn't move it and neither did I. We'd take care of it later, I was thinking. We'd clean it up when we got the chance, the Corvette back in motion, Jack gunning us out of there, saving his damage estimates for later. Right now you could tell what was ruined wouldn't keep us from speeding through the rest of the night.

Story Stories

I saw Bob Cook standing by himself behind the speakers that were singing "Twist and Shout." Holding a drink. Assessing the room as if it were empty. There were three hundred people massing and splitting, massing and splitting again, because at least half of them were busy reattaching themselves to as many old classmates as they could find in six hours. The fat and the bald. The gray and the tan. The fit and Bob Cook standing there like Jack Nicholson among the hotel guests in *The Shining*.

"Fitch," he murmured when I stepped carefully over the sound system wires.

"How's it going, Bob?" I said for a start.

Cook allowed a couple of beats to go by. He might have been waiting for the Isley Brothers to wrap up, but after ten seconds I was wishing I'd tripped over the speaker cables and said the hell with Bob Cook before I'd reached him.

"I'm in transition," he finally offered. "I'm between ships." He stared over my shoulder.

I heard the Ronettes start "Be My Baby." They sounded like they were singing from under the floor, and though common sense prompted that the recording was thin because we were behind the speakers, I was suddenly thinking somebody had turned the volume down so all the members of our class could learn what Bob Cook and I were talking about. I didn't blame anybody; I wanted to tell whoever it was to shut it off entirely because I couldn't understand it either.

"Bad question?" I said.

"No."

"Your wife here?" I tried.

"No." He lifted his glass, positioned it in front of his face as if he were remembering it was full of something with a bouquet. I wondered how I appeared through four inches of mixed drink, and then he lowered his glass to waist level again.

"Well, not the best of times or what?'

Cook watched me drain my drink. He might have meant to be generous, allowing me my excuse to pull away, a trip to the open bar both of us had paid for in advance. I jiggled the ice cubes. "Gin and tonic," I said, relying on the names for things like somebody who slept in a crib.

I held up the glass, but I kept myself from naming it. I said "Well" instead. The Ronettes were nearly finished doing their part to bring back 1963.

"Have a good one, Fitch," Bob Cook said as I retreated, back-stepping over those wires as if they had forked tongues, fangs, and rattles.

*   *   *   *   *   *   *   *

On Sunday afternoon, the class reunion fifteen hours behind us, I was happy to have Bob Cook to talk about with my wife when all of the Pittsburgh radio stations had faded, when we still had half the trip home in front of us with only top-forty, country, and evangelism up and down the dial. I let the radio run through *scan* one more time, but I was already saying "I'd guess Bob Cook if somebody asked me who should have gotten the prize for being furthest into outer space."

"Bob Cook," Laura said. "I talked to his wife while you were disappeared there for half an hour."

I watched Hollidaysburg inch along stoplight by stoplight; I saw Bob Cook staring over my shoulder, watching a strange woman sharing secrets with his wife. "What was she like?" I said.

"Fine. She was a whole lot easier to talk with than your classmates. She was just standing around like I was in a room full of aliens."

"Cook was out of it. He was burnt or something. He was wasted."

"He doesn't have a job," Laura said.

"I guessed that much. He was using code, but it wasn't that hard to crack."

"He left the Army."

"Twenty years and out."

"He didn't have twenty years."

"If he went in at the end of college, he had twenty years."

"She said he had eighteen years and ten months. She said he left early. Last October. Almost eleven months ago."

"Maybe he had his reasons," I said. "Maybe he was feeling guilty about becoming a double dipper."

"She didn't spell it out."

"Cook didn't even have an alphabet."

"She said enough as it was. What else should she admit to for her husband?"

"She could have spent the night keeping him moving. She might have led him round by the arm or something, kept him circulating for the six hours."

"They have a brain-damaged son. They have a daughter who's learning disabled."

"There's a difference?"

"Apparently."

I thought about the distinctions you'd make if both of your children were impaired, how you'd search for classifications, for fine tuning. Bob Cook had been in Vietnam; maybe he'd spent his tour in a cloud of Agent Orange.

"She said they're living with her parents in Pittsburgh."

"Old Bob Cook sounds like he's sliding down the tubes," I said. We were in Geeseytown, less than a hundred miles to go now. After a cemetery, a legion hall, and a closed gas station, we would be nowhere at all until Water Street where there were two closed stations and a Sunday flea market.

*   *   *   *   *   *   *   *

We reclaimed our children. We had a late dinner, and they let me talk about the reunion all the way through dessert. I flopped on the couch and had worked from Friday's paper, through Saturday's, and into Sunday's as far as Arts and Leisure, winding down, when the telephone rang.

"Fitch?" I heard.

"Uh-huh."

"Is this Fitch?"

"Yes."

"I don't have the wrong Fitch, do I?"

"I don't know."

"I think this is the wrong Fitch. You don't sound like yourself."

Whoever was trying to make a positive ID from a vocal lineup of Fitches hung up. I felt like Bachelors Number Two and Three, finding out I was somebody besides another person's fantasy because my voice didn't sound like it should, but I shut off the light in the kitchen before I looked outside to see if there was a strange car, shadows moving. The phone rang, again, and I began doing an inventory of things someone might demand from me.

"Hello," I said. There was someone sane who might be calling; it was ten-thirty, a while yet to the hour of the wolf.

"This is the real Fitch, isn't it?"

"I don't know."

"If this is the real Fitch, this is Bob Cook."

"Ok."

"I got your number. It took a while. I threw the damn thing away, and then I only remembered the name of your town without having the reunion program in front of me."

"You all right, Bob?" I said, a rhetorical question, what I might have asked if I knew I needed a prelude in order to hear a ransom demand. "Let me hear my wife's voice," I could just as easily have asked.

"Fitch, how do I sound to you? Do I sound like the old Bob Cook?"

"It's been twenty-five years, Bob. We don't know each other anymore."

"Give it some thought, Fitch. Think about it and let me know."

He hung up again, and I stood there wishing somebody had just described what he wanted to do with my wife's body or with mine. I wished I had just heard heavy breathing and the length and thickness of what the caller was stroking with his hand while he talked to me. I didn't want to think about whether Bob Cook was himself, or worse, whether I was the real Fitch.

He'd punched a girl in high school. That's what I remembered while I was waiting for the demons to tell Bob Cook to trial-run my number again. Cook had been the only guy I had ever seen slug a girl.

We'd been standing in the hall after lunch, a couple of minutes to kill before plane geometry. Maybe doing some furtive leering. Maybe just some dull sports-wish talk. Whatever we might have done with two minutes in tenth grade, and what I could see clearly was Sue Voller walking toward us looking good. "I hate her," Cook had muttered.

I didn't know how anybody could hate Sue Voller as long as he could watch her walk. I gave Cook a raised eyebrow and kept staring. "She spread stories about me to her friends," he said.

"What stories?"

"Story stories."

"She went out with you, Cook. I'm the one who ought to hate her. She turned me down."

But Bob Cook was all clenched teeth and reddening

face. "Hi, Sue," I said, ready to forgive any story she might have told about me.

She smiled. "Hi, there," she answered, maybe not even remembering she'd told me NO six months before.

"Voller?" Bob Cook had said.

It sounded so odd, she stopped. "Bob?" she said, as if she were trying to place him.

He stepped up to her and rammed his fist into her stomach, a solar plexus shot, doubling her up. "Oh," she breathed, all exhale followed by the silence you hear when somebody lands flat on his back. Cook ran, leaving me to explain to Sue Voller why I was the kind of person who'd hang out in the halls with a psychopath.

Nobody else had seen it happen. I didn't, five minutes later, think I'd seen it happen either.

Finally, then, the third call, fulfilling the omen. "Fitch," Bob Cook started, "we ought to get this over with."

"Sure," I agreed, calculating how close a sniper might need to be.

"Reunions are lies," he said, and I relaxed, moved, in fact, in front of the kitchen window.

"It's a given, Bob. We just leave the shit in our lives unspoken."

"I have problems with that, Fitch."

"Ok."

"I thought I remembered you, Fitch. I thought I recognized you last night. I thought you were somebody I went to school with."

I didn't answer. I decided that Bob Cook had used up his three tosses at the milk cans of sense.

"I'm not calling anymore, Fitch. You won't have to

wonder if I'm on the line the next time the phone rings.
It won't be me."

"Ok, Bob."

"Count on it, Fitch."

And for the rest of the night, at least, he kept his
promise; and the next morning, because all three of our
children were old enough to sleep through their last
week of summer mornings, I had breakfast with Laura, a
chance to fill in details for her about Bob Cook. "He's
not a curiosity anymore," she said. "Who are we dealing
with here?"

So I told her a couple of neutral anecdotes, reassur-
ances because I had to run through the Sue Voller fiasco.
She drank her coffee and looked like she wanted to answer the phone the next time Bob Cook called. "He's
done now," I said.

"Don't bet on it. This guy's a loony."

"He's depressed. The reunion made it worse. He
probably called ten people yesterday."

"He picked you, Doug. For some reason, he picked
you."

"Hardly," I said, but I agreed.

"What else do you remember about him from high
school?" Laura asked. "Maybe I'll hear a clue if you keep
the stories coming."

Other than things that wouldn't even leave
fingerprints, I could recall only one other Bob Cook
story:

"He was my lab partner in chemistry," I said. "I hated
chemistry. It was the only c I got in high school."

"Stick to Cook," Laura said.

I nodded. "You have to understand how numb I got in

chemistry, how little I remember from that class so you appreciate the specifics of this story."

"Fine. I understand that chemistry was not a good experience for you."

I was delaying my story. I'd thought of something to tell her, and now I was stuttering.

"Ok," I said. "One day during lab, right out of nowhere while we were heating compounds or whatever we did, Cook said to me, 'I've got a boner, Fitch.'"

Laura blinked as if I'd just turned on the overhead light, but I had things started now and kept on rolling: "Well, I just looked at him or something. After all, what do you say? and he said it again. 'I've got a boner.' And I really don't remember if I said anything then or not, but I know that what he said next was 'Don't you ever get a boner, Fitch?'"

Laura was looking through the doorway to check for our daughter. "What did you say to that," she managed.

"'Not in chemistry lab, Bob,' I remember saying. And then he said, 'Sure you do, Fitch. You get a boner in here.'"

Laura was staring at me now. "That's not the end, is it?" she said.

"That's it."

"No, it isn't. You're just embarrassed."

"Really. I think all I said was something like 'Why don't you go take care of yours?' and he didn't say anything else."

"You didn't tell your friends?"

"No."

"He never said anything like that again?"

"Sure he did," I said, surprised when I heard myself say it. "Maybe three other times. Always in chemistry lab, I think, so it got to where I tried to work far enough away from him he'd have to say it so loud even he wouldn't have that kind of nerve."

"You didn't think he was trying to lead you on?"

"I didn't think anything. I thought it was a stupid thing to be saying; you keep those things to yourself."

"He never said anything else afterwards?"

"He always started up as if he'd never mentioned it before."

"Well," Laura said, "at least he's married now. He's living with a woman."

"To tell you the truth, I never thought about it that way."

"Come on, Doug."

"Really. If I thought about it at all, it was sort of neutral, a kind of abstract horniness."

"How can you have abstract lust?" Laura said.

"It just seemed that way."

"Not a very good explanation, Doug."

"I suppose not," I said, signing off. I had to get to work. I had to get back to selling insurance to pay for all of the college expenses that were one year away from chewing up my income. And I was already tired of dealing with explanations for other people's lives. I had enough trying to account for myself, for three children and a wife I had to answer to. I was willing to be responsible for whatever totals I'd accumulate after another twenty-five years, give or take a decade, but the hell with Bob Cook, I was thinking, the hell with his boners and his retarded children and his out-of-work insanity. We'd been set into motion by the same community and the same high school, and all I wanted to do from here on in was go back and visit every ten years until my name went from the list of Classmates Attending to the list of Classmates Deceased. I wished him well; I wished him less pain. What else could Bob Cook expect from anybody listed on that program?

*   *   *   *   *   *   *   *

When the doorbell rang at eleven o'clock that night, I opened the door without thinking about whether or not terrorists were running spot checks on foolishness in our neighborhood. I lived in a small town in central Pennsylvania; I had a house on a street where the lawns blended into each other in color and texture as if there had been a communal decision to purchase identical seed.

At my door stood Bob Cook.

"Come on in," I said immediately, sounding like somebody who didn't wish he'd picked some other classmate to haunt.

"Fitch," he said, following me into the living room. "I'm only staying a minute."

I was relieved to hear that. I wanted to learn he had a reservation at the Holiday Inn in Allentown or Reading or Harrisburg, at least an hour more of driving in front of him; I wanted him to say he was on his way to Boston or New York or Baltimore and there was a natural reason for him to be pausing at my house before he disappeared.

And because I believed none of those things, I said "What's up?" to get the visit over with.

"I've been calling you," he said.

"Yes."

"I've been doing a lot of thinking since the reunion. I've been checking things over with our class."

"That's what reunions are for."

"Non-stop thinking, Fitch. Two days now. Thinking and calling, thinking and calling, thinking and driving here because thinking didn't seem sufficient."

"You want a beer? You want a drink?" Bob Cook was sounding like he needed at least ten beers to disconnect his circuits.

"Nothing like that, Fitch. I'm out of here in a minute. I'm back in the world."

"Ok." I badly wanted a beer, but I had a sense I was stuck on my couch until Bob Cook stood up again, getting out of the director's chair nobody in our family ever sat in. I wondered if Laura was listening from the room behind me, lying in bed in the dark and concentrating to discover who'd shown up so late, who was talking after eleven on a Monday night in our living room. The police, she'd think. She'd lie there worrying the police were delivering a sudden horror story—our older son a drug dealer, our younger son a thief, nude photos of our daughter in the wallet of her old social studies teacher from the middle school.

"I've been deceived, Fitch. I've been betrayed. You know what I'm talking about here? I've been thinking about how many lies a man can take before he's transformed into somebody else. Like being x-rayed too many times. There's a limit. You keep track of how many times your dentist has x-rayed you? You don't count until you feel a little polyp on your tongue. You don't keep track of lies either until you feel you're not yourself. I've been thinking about this for two days, and I'm not happy, Fitch. I've stopped being Bob Cook. I'm not who I was anymore." He paused. He stood up so suddenly I had to stay seated and look up at him from the couch like a child might if he'd just been caught carving FUCK on the legs of his fourth-grade teacher's chair, one letter per leg so the obscenity could be a year-long giggle.

"What do you think, Fitch? Do I seem like Bob Cook?"

"I don't know. Honestly. It's hard to get a grip on something like that so fast."

"My wife told your wife a lot of things about me, about my children. You think you know who I am now, but that's not enough, Fitch. You can never know enough about somebody to know who they are."

"I understand," I said, trying to pick the phrase that would defuse him. I was wishing very hard that Bob Cook would turn into somebody else right then and get in his car.

"Fitch," Cook said. He jammed his hands into his jacket pockets and stepped toward me, a combination of gestures so unnerving it made me sink back into the couch, bring my hands up in front of me. I knew, at that moment, why the victims of madmen in movies acted so foolishly, cowering and covering, giving themselves no chance to survive.

"You're one lucky son-of-a-bitch, Fitch," he said, backing up.

I was lost. I had to wait a breath longer, my hands still raised.

"Really, Fitch. So goddamned lucky." I saw he was heading toward the door, and I leaped up to follow.

"Your luck will change," I said, all congeniality and platitude.

Cook opened the door and turned to stand on the porch as if he were recreating his stance from five minutes before. "It would be somebody else's luck then," he said. "That's one thing I know for certain."

"Well, good luck anyway," I tossed his way, and I watched him get in his car, watched him pull out of my street, and watched for ten more minutes to make sure he hadn't turned around, intending to drift his car back into the lane with the lights extinguished and pitch bricks through my windows or set fire to everything I owned.

"It was Frank Miller," I told Laura when I had to go to bed or stand guard all night. She didn't answer. "Just Frank Miller from the office with a contract he didn't think could wait until morning," and she sighed and rolled over, asleep, I remembered, because she had an in-service day tomorrow, her first day back at work. If Laura could will herself to sleep at eleven as soon as her vacation ended, I thought, I could decide to let Bob Cook vanish.

In the morning, she was gone before I got out of the shower. I trusted my children to sleep until lunch, and I drove to work. The receptionist, when I passed her, said, "There's a man waiting in your office," and when I looked at her, she added "I hope I haven't inconvenienced you. He said you were old friends."

Bob Cook was looking at the art poster next to my desk, and I wondered what he was formulating from the not quite circular red ball hovering over what appeared to be the abstraction of a destroyed city. I didn't know the title of the work or the name of the artist; I'd picked it up ten years before because it had struck me as interesting one afternoon, and now it hung there like my routine job. Right then I thought that if Cook asked me to explain either one, I'd throw the poster away and resign.

But he was only getting something in order before he spoke. The poster could just as well have been an eye chart diminishing from large red E to an incomprehensible scramble of alphabet. "I found out you were never in Nam, Fitch. I checked it out, and you were never in country."

"That's right, Bob. But it's no secret. I could have told you that."

"You said you were. I took you at your word."

"When did I say that, Bob?"

"At the reunion."

I was cursing the receptionist; I was listing the excuses I could use to never attend another reunion. "The subject never came up, Bob. We hardly said anything to each other."

"Rick Davidson asked us to stand up if we were in Nam."

"Maybe he did. He asked us to stand up for a lot of things."

"You stood up for Nam, Fitch. You lied like some rotten scumbag."

"I stood up for having gone to Glenshaw Grade School. I stood up for living in Pennsylvania. I stood up for having three kids. I stood up for being in the Army once. Those are the things I stood up for."

"Fuck you, Fitch. I remember when you stood up for Nam because I was standing and twelve other guys were standing, and you were the only one I remembered ever knowing. All the rest were the guys who spent their high school locked in wood shop. I was thinking, 'That's who went to Nam. Wood shop guys. D-A haircut guys,' and then I said, 'There's Doug Fitch standing. Fucking-A, He was in Nam. Somebody with a brain besides me was in Nam.' "

"I don't know what to say, Bob. I wouldn't stand up for something like that unless I'd done it. I was in the Reserves, for Christ's sake; I was dodging and weaving to stay out of combat."

Cook went back to the poster, and for the first time I saw Hiroshima under that red sun. If Bob Cook stared at it a little longer, I'd be able to see the faces of survivors, their arms flung up to the heavens. If he stayed in my office for another ten minutes I'd be seeing boat people eating each other to stay alive, the end of life after the ozone layer dissolved in an acid bath of my daughter's aerosol sprays. "I'm disappointed, Fitch," he said. "Last night I had every intention of shooting you for lying about something like this." His eyes worked through the devastation in the poster. I thought I was going to throw up.

"I'm glad you didn't," I croaked. I might as well have been some idiot psycho-babbler spouting, "I hear some anger in what you're saying, Bob," and it seemed that Cook was seeing me clearly, that I didn't deserve that office, that the poster I had so carelessly bought and tacked up had been all along a scream of "Liar" or "Fraud" that I needed to address before justice emerged from the jacket pocket of somebody one hair further into dementia than Bob Cook.

"I decided it's more of a punishment for you to have to live with yourself."

It was a sentence I would have plea-bargained for on my knees. It freed me to start calculating how Cook could have confused me with somebody else standing up as proof of combat. What I remembered was the invitation to stand to show you were in the Army once had preceded the one about being in Vietnam. Maybe I hadn't sat down fast enough? Maybe I'd been looking around to see who all had managed to miss the Army altogether while Bob Cook was searching the room for a face he recognized? I might have stood for an extra second between questions and triggered the time release of Bob Cook's despair.

It was all I could find among the clutter so indifferently packed in my mind.

"I don't think I'll see you again, Fitch," he said then.

"I understand."

"Yeah."

I thought about whether or not I should make any gesture that might seem less than amiable, whether I should trust him to let me serve my sentence. "Fitch," he said, "you ever run anymore?"

"Run?" I said, as if he'd spoken in Cree.

"You ran in high school. You sprinted."

"I run from my car to this office when it's raining," I said, giddy with escape, but Cook didn't smile, so I added, "No, Bob, I know for a fact I don't sprint anymore. My hamstrings would snap."

"I know what you mean, Fitch, I gave it up myself."

I couldn't remember Bob Cook on the track team, not even in junior high school. I had no idea what he was getting at, unless it had something to do with establishing the common bond, the hope that conversation would luck onto something that resonated. And I wanted Bob Cook, as soon as he left, to find at least a

little bit of good fortune; I wanted to feel better about
anything I'd luck into by knowing his life was improv-
ing.

The Underground House

Jack's father always slowed when we passed the underground house. For the first ten years of school, all those grades when neither of us could drive and we had to go where our parents decided, maybe a hundred times I'd ridden with Jack's father past that house built into the earth like a bomb shelter, a half mile before the road both our families lived along crossed the turnpike. And each time he let up on the gas, as if Jack and I would naturally be fascinated for eternity by something that looked like the top of a parking garage, the level you were forced to park on if you went into Pittsburgh the Saturday before Christmas, stepping out into wind, snow flurries, and the fear that some mugger would shove you over the low curb, clutching your wallet while he watched you tumble five stories into the brass section of a Salvation Army band.

Everything I'd ever heard about the house I'd heard from Jack's father. How the owner was the kind of man who claimed that pretty soon we'd all be needing an underground house, that all of the skeptics and the lazy and the ill-prepared would end up crying on his roof, screaming to be allowed inside, something like the plot of any one of fifty films I'd seen since I was a kid.

I'd say it was probably 1950 when somebody would have set that story line into motion for the first time, one man thinking ahead and having his nightmare come true so everybody in the neighborhood showed up as soon as Armageddon started, saying, "Let me in. At least my family, at least my children." Close-ups of pre-schoolers and pregnant women, shots of the man with the cursed foresight debating with himself, a sort of contemporary Faust. All of the movies ended badly: the bunker-builder either lets them in and the collective collapses in over-crowded bickering, or he keeps them out and is driven mad by the horror of becoming exterminator. B movie stuff, but I never got tired of seeing the families reeling away to their doom, the crazed architect locked in the half-life of isolation. And three miles from where I lived there was this house constructed, for all I knew, before 1950, the first of its kind perhaps. For sure it was there in 1951, the year I'd started school, meeting Jack when he climbed onto the bus two stops down the road, and so the owner had been right on the cutting edge of thinking ahead before he'd gradually evolved from curiosity to ec-centric to simply ridiculous, squirreled away as if the leaps in megatons hadn't insured the end of defense.

Which included Jack's house, set back with a rutted driveway and unprepared for even conventional warfare, I was certain, because his father didn't bother to lock doors. "They get in anyway," he explained. "Burglars don't need an open door if they've set their minds to having your stuff." I couldn't argue with that, though it occurred to me that it was amateurs he was inviting, somebody like myself who, needing fifty bucks for the senior prom, might help himself to a wrist watch and a pair of earrings some afternoon.

On the television news, such petty disasters proliferated. The huge, irrevocable ones only weaved in and out of the reports like a sound track, and every time I was at Jack's house at eleven o'clock during our senior year, his father was watching from an old couch he'd moved to the basement, placing it so the first thing you saw from the top of the stairs was who was sitting there, what they were doing. The couch was all woven squares. It looked like an overstuffed lawn chair. It looked like somebody, Jack maybe, had been thrown against the back of it, loosening the frame so one end sagged in city streetcorner style.

In contrast; the television was new, set on a shelf above the bar Jack's father had built and he would sit so regularly on that couch, sipping whiskey while he watched, that after a while I counted on him being there, glass in hand, a couple of ice cubes jiggling around, making one of those incessant noises you start to associate with character, like the grinding of those steel ball bearings in *The Caine Mutiny*, Humphrey Bogart doing Captain Queeg showing everybody at the trial he'd lost control.

"Listen to this one," he'd begin, revving up as soon as Jack and I started down the stairs. Nobody watching the TV news could have felt more comfortable with analysis than Jack's father. He pointed out the reasons behind each story, even the brief spots about armed robberies in Pittsburgh or a two-car crash on the Parkway. "It's the unions," he'd say when the gunman was white. "They jack up the wages for doing nothing, and then the companies get even by laying off the short-timers and send them out to be thieves." If the holdup man was black, he was lazy, shiftless, looking for a quick fix. When the unfortunate drivers were men, he'd mutter "Drunk;" if they were women, they were irresponsible, incompetent, in the fog of conversation. After a while, you knew what was coming, something like a headache after you feel the first heaviness behind your eyes.

On the big stories, though, the ones that drew editorials, he rolled out commentaries that veered through attitudes like a slalom expert. He had a personal pipeline to their causes—like when the USS *Thresher* disappeared in April and the newscaster matter-of-factly announced its last verified depth as one thousand feet. "Lower," Jack's father said right away. "Who do they think they're lying to anyway?"

I didn't know. A thousand feet sounded deep enough to me, though for once I looked at the file films and listened to the Pentagon spokesman, deciding, on this one at least, Jack's father wasn't crazy because I could hear lunatic in the spiel of the Navy's shill, a statement prepared solely to mend anger. As if those 129 lost sailors were items a store had advertised and run out of before the sale was over.

I tried to guess why "Lower" sounded prescient. I waited for Jack's father to let loose with his rebuttal and thought about reasons for this fiasco all the way through the opening week baseball scores, the weather, and the five minute walk home as I cut through the yards where dogs didn't lurk on fifty-foot chains. I thought maybe I wanted to investigate this riddle myself, read the account in the *Press* the next day, but I let myself get tied up by the end-of-high-school knots, losing track of the *Thresher* news and practically everything else as I mailed in a college deposit, nailed down a union-driven summer job, and wasted myself at every early party I could slip into.

So it was the night before graduation, everyone taking a break, when I wandered downstairs during the late news, waving to Jack's father and receiving a salute from his whiskey glass, when I noticed, after a civil rights item from the Deep South that he snorted through, that the *Thresher* story had resurfaced in a feature showing photographs taken on the ocean floor where investigators had found the remains of the atomic submarine. The camera panned over all sorts of junk—metal plates, pipes, cable, an oxygen bottle—a regular archaeological dig that wouldn't add up, I didn't think, to 129 men if you gathered all of it and pieced it together in the basement of a museum.

In one sequence, the cameras showed a book. Lying open on the ocean floor, it looked like a personal calendar notebook a businessman might have on his desk. The newsman must have thought so, too, because he said, "And there it lies, what might pass for the diary of every black dream we've ever had, our collective nightmare," a preface to a commentary full of symbols: He said those sailors finally had experienced the horror of watching the edge of their universe fold in on itself a thousand feet down.

"Lower," Jack's father repeated. The ice cubes sang. "Lower, goddamnit. You hear what he said, fellows? You hear him say the sub was reporting 'Approaching test depth' when it got into trouble?"

We nodded.

He gave us a second to say more than field animals might. "Well, do you see what the problem is? Do you see why we're still lying?"

No, I thought, like a horse being saddled and accepting the weight.

"Figure it out," he said. "We can't let the Russians know how deep these things go. Let them think our submarine broke up at a thousand feet; let them think we can't build things right and then kick their asses from twice that depth where they'd never think of looking for trouble."

It sounded plausible, but I was thinking about the notebook lying open 8,400 feet below the surface, what it might say if it was being written in by one of the *Thresher* sailors at the time of the accident. "What would you write in your diary?" I asked Jack.

"Who'd stop to write?" he said.

I thought about whether or not I could hold a pen and make it form letters if the world was ending. "Don't you think you'd want to write something down to leave behind?" I said.

"I'd write my name," Jack's father broke in. "I'd make sure my name was down there on the page, and then, if I had the time, I'd tell the people that were worth it that I loved them." He took a sip of his whiskey; the announcer wrapped up the photo essay by saying, "The final message received from the *Thresher*, sent, almost certainly, after the submarine was doomed, was 'Exceeding test depth.'"

A few seconds later there was a film of somebody named Quang Duc burning himself to death in Saigon.

He was a monk, the newsman said, and it looked like he believed setting himself on fire would make a difference in whatever he was protesting. "Indochina," Jack's father said. "Where the hell they get this Vietnam stuff from? You think we ought to change the name of the United States? All those countries that change their names do is go to hell in a handbasket. The Belgian Congo. Look at it. Wait'll Cuba changes its name; wait'll there's hell to pay. Kennedy can't bluff forever."

I had to admit I didn't care much about the bonfire the monk had made of himself. I was waiting to see if they were going to have more clips of Christine Keeler and the rest of the whores that were threatening England, and I got my wish in the next story, paying attention to somebody's sold-to-the-networks home movie. "You boys learn to keep it zipped up," Jack's father said, "or you'll end up like all these politicians caught with their pants down."

*　　*　　*　　*　　*　　*　　*　　*

We slogged through graduation. We sat in the school gym because it rained like a punishment for our twelve wasted years, and there was nothing to do during the speeches but read the program to see what was happening to us all, half off to college, and half to the army or jobs, marriage and babies. I knew maybe ten people in the no-college half, guys who had ARMCO or Glenshaw Glass strapped across their shoulders. None of their names were on the back page where the scholarships and awards were listed except George Brethauer, American Legion Award to Highest General Student. I wondered what George was going to do with his prize, a book about Lincoln, when he reported to Camp Dix. I was listed as—Civic Club of Allegheny County—Exceptionally Able Youth—National Merit Competition— Letter of Commendation. Jack had scholarships from some women's group and Washington and Jefferson College. Even Ken Maier, the wrestler who was resting his hand on Angie Martin's thigh, was getting a scholarship from the Glenshaw Century Club.

By eleven o'clock there were maybe a dozen of us wandering around Jack's basement. I was trying to get my James Brown album on the stereo, but nobody wanted to hear *Live at the Apollo Theater* when they were drinking beer and groping for the girls who'd shown up. Somebody put the Fleetwoods on—"Mr. Blue"—and I could see girls like Angie Martin were melting for old stuff like that. She was limp, draped over Ken Maier, who was drinking while they danced as if he didn't feel those breasts pressed against him.

And then Jack's father turned the television on, settled back on the couch beside a couple who sat up to see the news beginning above the bar. The Medgar Evers killing was the lead story. I could tell, from where I was standing behind the bar, that the ice cubes were clinking against his glass, but I couldn't hear anything until after the first commercial break and nearly everybody had found an excuse to go upstairs.

A story came on from Canada. A policeman named George Lejda was trying to defuse a bomb while the cameras rolled. "There's lots of time on it," Lejda said, turning back to his work, and five seconds later it blew up.

"Shit," Jack said, "that guy's dead," but it turned out he'd only lost a hand.

"Well, what do you think?" Jack's father said then. "We got ourselves any chance in hell of being on the earth by the time your kids graduate? You want to fix any odds on that?"

I had to admit they seemed less promising than I wanted them, but I didn't know how somebody might actually set them, how he'd gather data and declare thirty to one, twenty to one, or something exotic like twelve to five. "I don't know," I said.

"I don't know either," Jack chorused.

"Look at this guy Lejda," Jack's father said. "You try to set the odds on that one. You figure a thousand to one, maybe. The guy's an expert; he knows what he's doing with that bomb or he wouldn't be fooling with it. Then you have to figure the odds on it being filmed, another thousand to one because you don't take home movies of every little bomb defusing. And then what do you have already but a million to one it blows up on camera so we get to see it."

"Sounds good," I offered. I was thinking about George Lejda and how he might have calculated his odds every day when he went to work as a bomb expert, but Jack's father wasn't finished with this one.

"Now," he kept on, "you figure how you just saw that little nightmare beat the odds, and you know right off the atomic war is a hell of a lot more likely. The big nightmare might be starting right this minute, Kennedy getting called, Kennedy getting raised, Kennedy sliding all of his chips into the pot and discovering his hand is nothing but a pencil-prick. The Russians aren't going to turn their ships around again; they've got Pittsburgh marked Ground Zero on every military map they own."

"Sixty to one," I said then. "It'll happen in 2023." I was using the logic of filming the holocaust from far enough in the future so I'd be dead according to the time lines I'd seen in the newspaper health columns.

"Odds don't tell you the date," Jack's father said. "Odds don't work the way you want them to." He looked back at the television where a commercial for Alka Seltzer was intoning "No matter what shape" and showing stomachs fat and thin, funny and so beautiful I wanted to lean into the screen and lay my head against the one in the bathing suit. "You ask George Lejda," he said, "if his hand was tearing apart in one million A.D. This time he took a good long swallow from his whiskey glass, which made me wonder if all along he'd been mixing his drinks with water.

"Hey," he said then, because the weather report was on, "you guys think you're drinkers. How about boiler-makers instead of mincing along with those beers you've had in your hands so long they're warm?" He poured himself a shot; he took three cans of beer out of the refrigerator, handed each of us one and stood the third beside the shot glass. I knew what a boilermaker was; I knew I didn't want one. But I was surprised he'd pin-set those beers for us because not once, while we'd been watching the news with him, had he ever offered us a drink. Carefully was how we'd been stealing from that bar for the past two years—no more than two shots from a bottle, never more than a beer apiece.

I watched a man point a stick at a line drawn through Pittsburgh. It was the cold front that had kept us in the gym; it was moving across Pennsylvania and taking its rain toward Philadelphia. "The hell with the boilermakers," Jack's father said, "let's have a Turkish chug."

I let Jack ask what a Turkish chug was, listened to his father explain how the pressure from pulling the tab opener forced the beer out the hole you had punched in the bottom of the can so you had to take in twelve ounces at once or slobber it all over yourself.

I wondered how the Turks had invented it since pop-tops were so new and clumsy I had maybe a dozen little slits in my thumb, fresh and old, from opening cans like a spaz.

"Let's do it," I said, and we took our Iron Citys and punched our holes and held the pop-tops until Jack's father said "Go," yanking so the beer exploded into our mouths and we had to swallow or choke, and I knew I wasn't going to stop unless I drowned under that can or was rescued, as it turned out, by Jack's father slapping his empty down on the bar.

I held my can sideways, trying to keep the half of it that was left from spilling out, but he was smiling at us. "Pussy drinkers," he said.

I couldn't argue with that. Beer was trickling over my hand; it was running between Jack's fingers. On the television the fluff story was about plans to bury a time capsule at the site of next year's World's Fair, right beside the one they'd buried in 1938, the last time there'd been a Fair in New York.

"What would you barflies put in a time capsule?" Jack's father asked.

Everything I thought of sounded foolish. All I treasured were records and magazines, cheeseburgers and pizza. I wanted my graduation program in there. I wanted to live inside that cylinder as if it preserved me somehow. I wanted to believe there would be somebody available to open my capsule in a hundred years.

"You chuggers know about the capsule in Oklahoma, the one with the car in it?"

Jack said "No" for both of us.

"Six years ago the state buried a Plymouth in Tulsa. They're going to dig it up in 2007."

"Why a Plymouth?" Jack prompted.

"They said it would last, that it would be appealing to whoever was there to dig it up in 2007 because it had style."

"They ought to get it out of there," Jack said. "They ought to get themselves a Corvette and junk that Plymouth before they embarrass themselves in the twenty-first century. At least New York has the sense to bury a new capsule so people in the future don't think we were as stupid as that stuff from 1938 must make us look."

Jack's father tossed back the shot he'd poured. "Don't spill too much," he said. "You're on KP in the morning."

He wasn't gone two minutes before the basement filled with drinkers like ourselves again. I tossed the ruined Iron City in the garbage; I opened another one and started weaving through the people I wouldn't see until our ten year reunion.

"It's over," Bob Craddock told me when I stopped in front of him. He was the non-college token, the only one there who didn't have some prize beside his name in the program.

"Roy Orbison," I said. "It's already spoken for."

"Roy Orbison doesn't know anything about over," Craddock said. "Over is everything, not just some stupid girl you can find another one of. Over is everything you've been doing for your whole life you can remember—classes, teachers, football, dances, the cafeteria, cruising—that's what over is."

"Go to college," I said. "Buy another four years."

"College is someplace else. I'd be gone. I'd be over anyway."

I thought Craddock was being as naive and stupid as was possible, and I agreed with every word. "Life truly eats shit," I philosophized.

Craddock beamed. "That's what I mean," he said. "That's what over is all about."

"You get yourself some catalogs," I said. "Get some applications out." For the first time in my life, I saw Angie Martin sitting by herself. I wanted to open her blouse and spend the rest of the night with my face on her breasts so the memory of them would be indelible.

I dropped beside her on the old couch. "Angie," I started, but she was singing, "It's my party and I'll cry if I want to, cry if I want to . . ." I wondered how anybody, even Ken Maier, would be tempted to try another body if he had this one beside him. I knew I was willing to try teaching her to think enough to fill in the cracks between attacks of lust and subsequent fulfillments.

She looked like somebody wishing she was selling Girl Scout cookies again. "Angie," I managed to repeat, and she kept on with Leslie Gore, stuck on the chorus, and I was convinced I could undress her while she sang or at least whisper every act I wanted to perform on her so she'd call me the minute she came out of this spell, giving me the time and the place to start down my wish list. I alphabetized. I got them all in an order I could repeat, the small explosives of each word ready to spiral down her auditory canal, and then Ken Maier was bellowing from the top of the stairs.

"Who you talking to, asshole?" he shouted down at me. He looked like he might have a gun, like somebody who'd leap and land on me.

"Lolita," I said. "Sue Lyons."

He wasn't getting it. He was hunched down so his shoulders looked like they were getting ready to support the planet.

"Leslie Gore," I shouted, and when Angie laughed, he took a stride meant for level ground and fell face-first down the stairs so I could see the clench of his teeth all the way down to the basement floor.

"Oh shit," Ken Maier said, staring, for all I knew, at the patterns in the tile. "Oh shit," he said again, kicking his legs on the bottom step to show he wasn't paralyzed, that he was working up the coordination to come over and rip my tongue out.

Angie Martin was up then. She was bending over him and saying "Ken" in a way that made me want to plunge out an upstairs window while she waited for me to thunk onto the lawn.

It took Jack five minutes to get Ken Maier into his car and put Angie Martin behind the wheel. "You get him home, ok?" he was saying.

"Sure." She didn't look like anybody who could maneuver a car through anything more challenging than an empty parking lot. I wanted Jack to ferry Ken Maier, leaving me to drive Angie home. Leslie Gore, I kept thinking, some Sarah Lawrence girl, some swimsuit heiress who nobody but Angie Martin would listen to by next summer. Like Annette. Like Little Peggy March.

Jack was giving her hand signals to help her with the driveway. It had a ditch on one side where the road he lived on had eroded for years, deep enough now to keep a tire prisoner until a tow truck arrived.

As soon as she managed to miss the small cliff, Jack said, "Let's get the hell out of here, go someplace."

"Sure."

"Let's do a township tour, see what we're leaving behind."

"Angie Martin is what we're leaving behind," I said.

I wasn't sure where Jack wanted to go, but as long as I had another beer to open each time I finished one, I didn't much care because I could tell he was keeping to his itinerary, circling through the connect-the-dots of memory north of Pittsburgh, turning the car into something like one of those little overbred dogs you see spinning themselves around and around and around just to find a place to take a shit on their owners' lawns.

Finally, we were in Cherry City, one of those places where the students in our class who weren't going to college were concentrated. This was where the couples who were serious in the halls lived, where they got married two weeks after graduation and had three quick babies and lived upstairs in one of these three story brick houses that, for all I knew, were designed to hold three generations of the same family so you simply moved your stuff down a flight of stairs every twenty years or so, finishing on the ground floor or even in the basement, listening to the squall of your great-grandchildren come wailing down the staircases to where you were sitting out the last years of your life. "I lived here once," Jack said, attacking my metaphor. "We moved the summer before first grade."

The only thing I knew about Cherry City was it had a reservoir and a baseball field that lay just below it, so when Jack said, "What now?" after he'd looped the short streets twice. I said, "The old ball field."

I went out to stand at home plate to try and get a sense of how it had felt, six years before, batting against Mike Kushon, the big kid with the August birthday so he was two weeks from thirteen and his first mustache, yet still pitching for the Cherry City Dairy Queens. The week before I'd had to bat against him he'd pitched a no-hitter that made the *Pittsburgh Press* because he'd struck out all eighteen batters. He'd struck out the first four batters in our lineup, so he had at least twenty-two in a row when he hit Charley Schneider, who batted right before me, in the middle of his ear flap. There'd been this little thump, softer than I would have guessed for the cause of permanent injury. I'd watched Charley Schneider grab his ear and sit down in the dust, not budging from the batter's box while the coaches crowded around and he tried to stop crying long enough to tell them about his pain. It took them maybe five minutes to pry Charley's hand away from his ear, and I leaned forward to see how much blood he'd cupped in his palm, whether or not he'd hear anything when somebody screamed in his ear.

I was praying that he'd sit there crying until it got dark when the manager pulled me aside. "Don't step in the bucket now," he cautioned. "Don't give in just because he let one get away." The coaches had Charley up and on his way to first base while the parents applauded and I dug in to flail at the first pitch. I wanted to get it over with, three fireballs that might not kill me, and what happened was I'd bailed out with my back foot, stuck the bat out, and blooped one just over first base for a double that pushed Charley Schneider ahead of me with his hand glued to his ear. "Way to hang in there," I heard. "Way to swing that big stick." Charley didn't look like he heard anything but the echoes from the inside walls of a bee hive.

I thought maybe I could reach the woods in center field now if Mike Kushon had stayed twelve and was pitching instead of working at Goss Gas and drinking underage at the Mt. Royal Inn. I'd be able to stride into a pitch instead of inching back toward the catcher until my backswing hit his mask. "You ought to stand in the outfield if you want to fantasize," Jack suggested.

"I never liked defense," I said. "I only played third base so I could get to bat again," close enough to the truth if you could cross-out Mike Kushon from the rotation.

"You ought to go to centerfield, go out there and back up so you're at the edge of those woods. It gives you a different angle on the game; it lets you see exactly where the perfect swing might get you so you know where your limits are."

"I can see my limits fine from here," I lied. From where I was standing at home plate, it looked like those trees were reachable, that my perfect swing against a grade school pitcher would arc a ball into the oaks that stood behind the first scrub rows of sumac.

Jack didn't care whether I went out to stand in centerfield or not. He started up a path that, when I followed, diminished to burdock and thistle and poison ivy.

I knew we were floundering toward the reservoir, and when I stood beside Jack at its fence he acted as if he'd just remembered why he'd been driving for the last forty-five minutes. "Let's go swimming," he said, ignoring the barbed wire at the top of the fence.

I was glad to see it because the wire looked impenetrable enough to keep me from having to make up excuses to avoid jumping to my death if the water was more than six feet deep. There wasn't any shallow end to this pool, no inner tubes to climb aboard and paddle around as if you were bored with swimming instead of terrified of the unlucky tumble into deep water.

Jack climbed anyway, getting to the barbed wire so fast I saw myself on the news, a blow-up of my senior picture, a shot of a body bag being slid into a police ambulance. "Graduation Tragedy," the promo would say. I curled my fingers through the loops of fence and pulled myself up so my face was even with the woven barbs. Jack was testing the barbed wire like a mass murderer who didn't care if the guard had him in his sights. "Shit," he was saying, proving he still had brain cells, and then I climbed back down to life because I knew he wasn't going to rake himself through that tangle.

When we left the reservoir, Jack drove to the underground house. "I want to get inside," he said. "I want to say hello to the goofball who's been locked inside ever since we moved out of Cherry City."

There wasn't any barbed wire on the edge of the roof, but I was thinking land mine, booby trap, and guard dog while I walked as softly as I could on the gravel and tar and cement. In the darkness I listened to Jack sending signals into the house below us by kicking the roof. I was holding my breath, and here was Jack delivering a message full of the end of civilization. I tried to remember Morse Code, the dits and dahs of the alphabet; I tried to follow Jack's thumping to hear if it was coherent or if he was simply sounding out the panic of someone about to be irretrievably radiated. Wouldn't someone as prepared as the mole below us be listening twenty-four hours a day to his ceiling, waiting to be fulfilled?

Jack switched to jumping, jamming his heels down hard. There was nothing left to debate about the system of his noises. I began to jump. I wanted the albino to cackle "I told you so." I wanted his pink eyes glued to the television, expecting Conelrad to break in with the doomsday report. I wanted to crack right through the roof and put a deadly hole in the defense system.

As soon as I got tired enough to think again, I said, "Where's the door?" I hopped down and started working the perimeter, left to right, Jack still jumping but following my lead, staying with me until, on the side away from the road, I found a set of seams, a handle, a depression in the ground so the door could swing out and you could get in without dropping to all fours.

I kicked it a few times. I pounded with both fists as if the first mushroom was forming on the horizon, as if Pittsburgh and its steel mills were churning up to heaven like so many indecipherable fragments. Jack positioned himself right over where the hallway or foyer had to be and bounced. We were screaming now. I yelled "Open up!" until it turned into a series of long vowels that wavered with my footwork. When, at last, the vowels shortened and stopped, so did we.

"We're dead," Jack said, landing beside me. "We're

absorbing thousands of rems a minute; we're balding zombies."

"We throw up. We have diarrhea."

"We have sudden weakness and chills."

"We lapse into coma."

"We join eternity."

"Sure we do."

"And this asshole opens his door in five years and tries to guess which one of the skeletons in his backyard was the last guy to scream 'Open up!'"

"Sure he does."

"And then he names himself king."

I was thinking how we were working up all the symptoms just fine without any help from the Russians. I stood there beside Jack for another minute, but nobody answered the door. We drove back to Jack's house. We sipped the last two beers we had in the car, and I decided to sleep the night off at Jack's. I wasn't going home to wake up with the heaves while my mother listened outside the bathroom door. Let her guess. Let her assess my stupidity by extrapolating what she'd been observing for the past eighteen years.

Which was fine, except when we got back downstairs, empty and quiet unless you counted the needle jerking at the center of "Shake a Tail Feather," Jack said, "One more Turkish chug."

"Christ, no."

"Without my old man. One on one so we can see if somebody can actually get to the bottom."

"What the hell," I caved in.

"Exactly."

I yanked my tab, opened my mouth, and the can flushed itself down my throat. I slammed the empty down and said "There," although it didn't matter because Jack was holding his can against his chest and letting the beer run down his shirt, saying "I don't know how anybody can do it."

"It's a worthless talent."

"Sure it is," he said.

Suddenly I felt compelled to take off my shoes and my pants and sit on the old couch, trying to remember what came next. Sleep, I conjured, and I let myself slump back to the consequences of more beer than I'd ever had. I started to stare at my thumb. It had a new slice in it from the pull top, one more paper cut facsimile, as if my parents might believe I spent so much time handling office supplies I'd be permanently scarred.

I don't know if Jack watched me meditate or whether he went to his room or just upstairs to the living room couch, but he'd turned out the lights, because when the funnel cloud of dizziness and nausea roared in from wherever the weather of evil habits originates, I lurched up in blindness and I had to get myself moving or else I'd be cleaning up vomit and hearing Jack's father retell the story of my weakness forever.

My stomach settled as I shuffled in the dark, finding a wall, a door, the one that opened to the garage. I felt my way from hood to trunk, and by the bumper I could see again, the garage door open, the early morning still in primeval black.

I was starting to feel as if I wouldn't puke. I was thinking that if I stood there in the driveway for a few more minutes I was going to use the three A.M. air so well it would deserve its place among the cures listed in the book of quackeries. Halfway up the driveway I noticed a

stain on the asphalt that looked like the shape of the
universe, the Great Saddle, and when I bent down to
confirm it, my head sloshed so heavy it toppled me forward into darkness.

"Shit," I heard, coming up from the toxic waste of
unconsciousness. "Shit, we about fucked you up for
good." Bob Craddock was bumping my head against the
rear left tire of his car, dragging me by the feet from
under it.

I sat up then, shaking off sludge, and took a good look
at where I'd been sprawled under that car. "That was one
lucky alignment you had there," he said, and I had to
rubber stamp that, seeing as how they'd backed over all
the bare space on either side of my body so the rear tire
had been squatting inches from my slobbering mouth.

"I think I saw your elbow or something. It was just
enough to make me scream 'Stop!' at Bobby because I
don't think we were quite backing up straight." Angie
Martin was looking down at my underpants. "It was one
lucky chance," she kept going, "that we had the ditch
here to miss so I was looking out the side window like
Jack showed me tonight." She was leaning against Bob
Craddock, who, it appeared to me, had parked his car in
Jack's garage after he'd picked up Angie Martin from
wherever she'd called when Ken Maier had turned use-
less.

The coincidence series, I thought, like the lottery long
shot of two men in a silo cranking up their share of nuclear warheads. It was possible, I was imagining right
then, that you could sit down with a friend and just for a
goof start dialing numbers in tandem and get something
launched. If Bob Craddock could sleep with Angie

Martin, I could have a vision of warheads going off; if I could pass out so perfectly close to crippling or death, I might be the one who finds the secret entrance to the underground house. What the hell, I thought. It's my luck. I could use it up whenever I needed to, and if it was gone now, so be it. I wasn't going into the steel mills; I wasn't going into the army. I didn't need luck to keep from frying in molten metal or tearing apart above a Bouncing Betty. I sat there at the feet of Bob Craddock and Angie Martin and thought about how it would feel if you were a half mile inside the earth and the wall may or may not buckle in on you.

I was ready to stand up. I heard whisperings from all over the yard as if everyone I'd ever heard who had died had rushed up to see my corpse and were backing off now, mumbling and cursing. I kept sitting there, waving Craddock and Angie Martin back inside his car and watching them drive off into the first dark blue of the morning sky. Once the car dropped over the first hill, I could hear myself think, pick out the voices of every teacher I'd had since I was six, from Mrs. Spangler to Miss Corda, and all of them had their words tied up in balloons over their heads so what they had to say stayed suspended for me to read. So I had plenty of time to take it in, see if there was significance to any of it, give them a grade maybe, for what they'd said and how they'd said it.

On The Radio

"This is Archie," Gene's father said.

Gene thought Archie looked out of whack, even for a man in a wheelchair.

"Did you hear me?" his father said. "Say hello to Archie."

"Hi," Gene tried, working out in his head while he said it—how Archie could have inverted his elbow as if the hinge of it were nailed on backward.

Archie grimaced and swiveled in his chair, and Gene was just starting to think his father would begin to scold him for not replying when Archie managed to squeak, "Hi there, fella."

Gene was relieved. He'd been expecting flying spit, maybe even drool down the chin, but Archie had pulled through with only a little boy's voice that was reasonably clear. One arm even seemed to work fairly well. Archie used it to push a button on the chair, turning it toward an elaborate ham radio set.

"Archie made this whole thing," his father explained while Archie was busy activating some controls. "He's a regular genius with this stuff. Ask him about it. You'll never stump him."

Gene had seen a set-up like this one at Bill Nelson's house, which had only been a block away before they'd moved last year. Every Saturday Gene had delivered a coffee cake and two loaves of bread to Bill Nelson, and he'd gotten used to watching Nelson working the dials specially made for the blind, how Nelson could fine tune everything by touch and sound.

"That's England," Nelson had said once. "That's my cousin from the big island."

Gene had nodded and listened, but Nelson's cousin was just talking about the weather, how cold it was for June. It could just as well have been one of Gene's uncles five miles away talking about how the beans were going to be late this year.

Eventually, Bill Nelson would say "How much?" although for months it was always $1.27—sixty-nine cents for the maple nut cake, twenty-nine cents each for the sandwich white breads. Nelson would open a change purse and start fingering coins, getting four quarters together before he'd start on the dimes and nickels and pennies. Gene had always wondered why he didn't use five quarters, but Bill Nelson had never missed giving him the right change, pressing it into Gene's hand while voices identified themselves on the radio.

"Glaucoma," Gene's father had said once. "Bill Nelson used to be a hell of a man, but you can't muscle up for glaucoma."

Now they delivered leftover rolls and coffee cakes to this charity home on Saturday nights. The stuff went bad in two days. "There'd be nothing we could do with it on Monday," his father said. "We've got to sell it or give it away the next day. It's not like cookies or layer cakes."

Gene knew his father had picked this home because The Prince lived here. There was a home like this one just as close to the bakery, but when The Prince had moved in here right about the time they'd bought a new house, they'd started dropping off two or three flat pans of baked goods after closing time on Saturdays, his father hiking upstairs to visit The Prince for a few minutes.

But they'd been delivering about-to-be-stale sweet rolls to the St. Barnabas Home for six weeks before his father had told Gene who the old man was that they visited upstairs. Even then, an accident: "Who was that masked man?" Gene had asked finally as they rode home in the station wagon.

His father had used his straight-through-the-windshield stare for a while so Gene would know the next words should be memorized. "It's not a joke," he'd said after a half mile.

"It's too boring to be a joke," Gene had said, "sitting around in that little room while you talk to some old guy who stinks as bad as that cheese you give him."

"Limburger."

"Whatever."

"He likes it."

"So he likes it."

"He's your grandfather."

"Him?"

"He's The Prince."

"The masked man?"

"They're all the same."

Gene had been hearing about The Prince off and on for years, but always secondhand because the name came up between his parents at dinner or someplace. His family didn't elaborate; they didn't ask questions that demanded revelations. It had taken Gene another trip to the home, his learning that the place was for charity cases who had to give up even the couple of shirts they owned to St. Barnabas before they'd be admitted: "So what'd he do so bad?" he'd finally asked. Every other grandfather he knew would have moved in with one of his kids if he ran into tough times.

"He drank. He stole. He wrecked everything he ever touched while he went on living like a prince. Your mother even did his job for him when she was in high school. She went down to Locust Street with your aunt no matter what time of year and swept his floors and carried his ashes and shoveled his walks while he slept it off somewhere."

Gene had tried to picture his mother carrying buckets of ashes, maintaining a coal furnace for the Locust Street School, but he'd had trouble with that one. His aunt he *could* see. She was still intimidating at fifty; he was still wishing for biceps like hers.

He'd known that that was as much explanation as he'd probably get from his father, who specialized in implications, but he'd heard a few things from his mother, how his aunt had kicked dozens of drunks out of the house after she got out of high school and started in being a secretary for the Bureau of Mines, living at home so her salary was worth something besides room and board. His aunt had even stayed living there after The Prince was gone, after Gene's mother was gone and there weren't any drunks to threaten with a broom except old man Cordesich from next door who played a concertina and sang songs in Croatian when he drank.

The biggest surprise she had for Gene now was how well she could sail stones across the yard and hit the cats that slipped through the hedges to stalk birds, but she was willing to talk sometimes and Gene had started sorting things out better. He'd started putting old Prince stories together with his aunt and his mother and even his grandmother, who had always looked to him as if she'd been unmarried for life.

All of this finding out was more awkward than confusing because now, after never asking why he had only one grandfather even though the question seemed obvious, Gene had begun to track down the Prince's life like a detective, making the rounds of his relatives, singling them out when they were apart from each other to squeeze eyewitness stories out of each of them.

His aunt, so far, was the best storyteller, especially when she began by saying "You want to hear about The Prince again? That old stew. There's not enough time in the day to tell stories about that pantywaist."

She'd whale one of the rocks she kept on the bannister, kicking up dirt a couple of feet from a crouched cat. If she missed by too much, the cat wouldn't move, just turn and groom itself for a moment. That wasn't very often, but she'd let Gene give it a try if the cat didn't bolt. One time he'd plunked one in the back and the squall had stayed with him ever since; his aunt had clapped him on the shoulders and said "Good pitch."

Her best story was about The Prince falling from a silo, tumbling drunk into the lucky haystack. She'd told it to him for the first time right after she'd hit a gray striped cat in the throat so it hadn't even run, just buckled and sat for a few seconds with its head down like it was choking. They'd watched it until it crept into the hedges and then his aunt had said, "He ended up like Little Boy Blue when it was time to blow his horn, the old pantywaist. So drunk he fell like a baby. Nobody else would get out of that fall without so much as a scratch— seventy-five feet. What was that old stew doing hanging outside on the top of that thing?"

It was the end of The Prince working on that farm. Nobody wanted the liability problems of having a drunk for a field hand. Gene's grandmother had asked him to leave five years before, so he'd walked off to do flagman or short order cook or dishwasher, whichever one came next on the resume his mother had recited for him once.

Now, standing here watching Archie lurch in his wheelchair, Gene thought The Prince would have ended up like this, arms and legs bent backwards by the force of falling, but he had no more idea of why Archie jerked around like he did than why The Prince drank and tumbled off a silo, hitting the softest target on the farm like a stunt man.

"Can you call China?" Gene said, feeling stupid as soon as he asked.

"Don't know the lingo," Archie said.

"How about Russia?"

"Same problem." Archie shot backwards then as if catching himself too close to the edge of an observation deck with a low railing.

Gene was thinking that ham radios were probably illegal in Russia and China, that Archie was treating him as if he were a child version of one of the 80 IQ guys who ended up in a place like this because they weren't dumb enough to qualify for special treatment. "You better be smart or stupid in this world," his father would say every time he watched the news. "You better be rich or poor."

"I'll be back down in a little while," his father said now. "You can visit with Archie. Maybe he'll let you talk on that thing."

"Ok," Gene said, and turned back to Archie, asking, "How about Canada?" giving him an easy one so something would get going on the radio. "How about somebody way up north in Canada?"

"Sure thing, fella," Archie said. He started working some dials, but all Gene heard were squeals and machine guns. "Lot of interference tonight," Archie said.

Gene's father popped back through the door and waved him out of the room. "Be back in a minute," he said to Archie.

"Sure thing, fella. I'll have the North Pole on here for you in a minute."

His father was holding something in each hand. "I forgot the limburger," he said. "Had to go back to the car and get it."

"We don't want to take it home with us, that's for sure."

"The Prince wants to see you," his father went on. " 'How's Ruthy's boy?' he asks. "

"Mom doesn't visit. Why should I go up there?"

"She had to live with him. You don't. He's an old man; he's your grandfather; he can't do anything anymore but good for you."

"You didn't even tell me who it was when I was sitting there smelling that cheese for an hour."

"You always knew who The Prince was. You can't make me think you didn't know."

"I never knew. How would I know?"

"What would we be doing visiting the same old man in a charity home week after week?"

"I don't know. I never thought about it. You're *always* doing something for charity."

His father turned sideways to him so he was in profile against the twelve dozen bear claws and maple rolls sitting on the kitchen shelf. The implication expression was forming and fading on his face, not quite setting in to force Gene upstairs where he hadn't wanted to go since he'd found out he was supposed to be interested in The Prince.

"Why doesn't he just walk down here with you?" Gene said. "I wouldn't run away or anything."

"He doesn't get around so good."

"He eats down here. He wants to see me so bad he'd come down here once in a while." He was inspired, Gene thought, his logic unarguable.

His father turned back toward him and handed Gene a bar of soap that had been carved into an animal. "He thought you'd like this."

"What is it?"

"A buffalo. See?" His father traced the outline of the head as if he were blind.

"I guess. Why'd he think I'd want a soap buffalo?"

"Because you're twelve. Because you're a boy. What else does he have to go on only seeing you a few times?"

"Tell him I'm visiting Archie this time. Tell him Archie's got somebody from way up north in Canada on the radio for me to talk to."

"I'll tell him that next trip you'll stop in."

"Tell him the buffalo's great."

"Good."

His father backed up a step, then another, turning so he slipped behind the counter with the rolls on it. Gene noticed there were a few coconut ones mixed in with the maples. "Archie's a smart man," his father said. "Inside that wreck of a body he's a lot smarter than you'd think. That's why Brother Paul lets him work with the radio behind the kitchen; he needs something besides what takes care of the other men here."

Gene rubbed at the buffalo's back, seeing how much pressure it took to erase the detail. "How could anybody eat limburger?"

"With onions."

"Like a sandwich?"

"Or like fruit on cereal."

"Like somebody died and got left out in the sun."

"So you take care of Archie. You go in there and make his evening for him by listening to that radio. He'll be tickled."

Instead of going right back in when his father left, Gene stayed in the kitchen. He didn't want to get back to Archie before there were any Canadians talking from the Arctic Circle; he didn't want to get there and find Brother Paul, the Home's Director, waiting to make suggestions about the best way to train his soul. His father never seemed to notice the way everything Brother Paul said was something cut out of a sermon.

"Your father could do worse than pass his good works on to his son," Brother Paul had said to Gene once. "May you be so blessed." He looked around now to see if somehow Brother Paul might be watching as he fished out one of the coconut rolls and walked among the sinks and ovens eating it. There was no other sign of food. Everything was metal and clean; every door to a cabinet that he tried was locked. He ended up back at the bakery pans, thinking about a second roll but then turning it down, looking instead at the brown filling jammed between the toes of the bear claws and remembering how he'd learned a few months ago that it was made from ground up stale cakes and rolls, that his father tossed all of the scrap into the mixer with some water and turned it into sweet roll and coffee cake filling. "It's just sugar and flour," his father had said. "What else would you put in filling anyway?"

Gene had watched the dried rolls churning around in the mixer; he'd tried to guess which kind would drown last, going down and coming up indistinguishable from the rest of the pulp. It looked as if they didn't have to drive all of those trays out to St. Barnabas on Saturday, but Gene hadn't asked; he thought maybe a little of that goop went a long way, that his father stored it for weeks until he had to whip up another batch.

He tried a different door than the one he'd entered by and ended up in the dining hall where the tables were arranged in four long columns, maybe twenty men to a side. Gene wondered if Brother Paul and the other monks ate at a separate table, whether or not they said a prayer before they let the men get to work on the food. The Prince didn't sound like he'd be very interested in putting up with Brother Paul saying grace, but maybe this place changed you somehow. He counted the place settings to see how close his guess was. There were bowls and cups already laid out for the next morning's breakfast. There were eighteen bowls on one side of the table, and when Gene finished counting he tried to imagine The Prince sitting there tomorrow eating oatmeal. He thought of Archie fumbling his spoon and having to ask the attendant to pick it up.

"Rolled oats," his father had said once, when Gene had asked him what they'd get for breakfast in a place like this. "Or square egg."

Gene had known the pain of oatmeal, the dogfood look of it even with sugar sloshed thick on top; he'd had to ask about square egg.

"You know, powdered eggs. They fix them in big tins and cut the portions in squares like you would a sheet cake."

"Any good?" he'd asked, even though he'd known immediately how hideous it had to be.

His father, for once, agreed. "Count yourself lucky," he'd said, "if you don't get a taste of it. Sometimes they're not even yellow. They can get like bad margarine, the color all funny shades that lets you know they can't be good. You don't remember oleo, how white it was, like lard, and then they added a kind of smeared-on yellow so it ended up looking like a bad color television picture."

That explanation had more detail than his father had ever given about The Prince except for one story about his mother's high school prize money, five silver dollars she'd won for being the best bookkeeping student at Etna High.

"It was one of the last straws. Your mother was seventeen and The Prince had already stolen from everybody else in the house, but never from her. Even so, she had the five silver dollars wrapped in a handkerchief and under a sweater in her drawer.

"One day they were just gone. Maybe he'd stolen them a week before. What did she know for sure not checking every day, but she sure as shootin' knew where they'd gone to when they turned up missing.

"'Ruthy, Ruthy,' The Prince said after he'd been found out. 'You're my baby; I don't steal from my baby.' But he couldn't keep that song and dance up for long, knowing there wasn't any doubt.

"Your mother was crushed. Prize money—her father had stolen prize money, something she'd really earned."

Gene put the buffalo beside one of the bowls, lining it up so the eyes, if they'd been carved well, would be looking into the bowl tomorrow morning at milk-sopped oatmeal. He brushed the coconut crumbs off his hands and made his way back through the kitchen to the room where Archie was listening to static.

Archie swiveled in his wheelchair and almost pitched over the armrest. He smiled. "You ready to talk to Santa Claus?" he said.

"Tell him I want to grow six inches," Gene said so Archie had a chance to laugh. An attendant, Gene noticed, was in the room now, and Gene thought maybe Archie's radio time was about up, that the white shirt/white pants man was here to haul Archie away for the night.

"Got to hurry a little," Archie said, jerking his better elbow toward the man leaning against the far wall. Gene nodded and listened to the background noise on the radio, hoping he'd hear a few recognizable words before Archie's curfew.

"You know Gottlob Lang?" he said.

"Sure I do, fella. He's a crusty old kraut."

"Anybody around here ever call him The Prince?"

"No, can't say that they do, but that doesn't mean it's not done. How come you want to know so much all of a sudden about old Lang?"

"He's my grandfather."

Archie jerked his elbow again. "That right?" he said. "Well, that beats it all for sure. You don't see much of him, do you?"

"No."

"That surely does beat everything. Old Lang a grandpap to anybody on the face of this Earth."

Archie nudged a dial and got a whistle out of the radio. "He punched holes with his bare hands through my grandmother's living room walls once," Gene said, and when Archie nudged a second dial to stop the whistle, he went on: "He brought home a bunch of live chickens he won in a card game and threw the sack of them in the bedroom so they all got out and went crazy in there."

"Old Lang was a real drinker in his heydey, wasn't he?"

"The best," Gene said. "The Prince of Etna. He wrecked six cars and never got hurt. He fell off a hundred foot silo and didn't even break an arm."

"Prince Lang, then, is it?" Archie said. "He carves soap all day in that room of his."

"He's eighty-years-old and still gets around."

Archie found some voices then and Gene shut up, listening to see what they were saying, where they were saying it from. "We have somebody here," Archie said, though Gene couldn't make anything out of it. "We have somebody from up North where you wanted them."

Things cleared then, and Gene heard somebody saying "Newfoundland Nat here, looking for somebody who's in the sunshine." Archie swiveled in the chair, jerking his elbow again, a sign, Gene thought, for him to get in closer and man the controls so he could talk to Newfoundland Nat.

"Hear that?" Archie said. "You want to talk to Newfoundland? That's North; that's almost as good as Santa Claus."

"A cousin," Gene said, trying to make Archie laugh again, but suddenly Archie flopped forward as if he'd been leaning on a fence that had snapped, pitching face-first half way to the floor before he was caught by a harness of rope Gene hadn't noticed.

"Unhh," Archie said. "Unhh." And he dangled there in a tight V gone sideways like the signs for "Greater Than" or "Less Than," Gene never quite certain which was which.

The attendant materialized as if the ropes, when taut, triggered an alarm, "Archie, Archie," he said, pressing him upright, but Archie didn't look any better for it, his neck so slack Gene thought maybe he'd snapped it when the ropes took hold.

"Archie's out of it for tonight," the attendant said to Gene. "We're going to have to put him to bed."

Gene worried for a few seconds about the collective pronoun, but the attendant went ahead and wheeled Archie away by himself so Gene had nothing to do but sit down in front of the radio and wait for his father, glad he didn't have to ride the freight elevator to the second floor or the third, following the chair down the hall to whichever room was Archie's.

Archie had seemed to know a lot about what The Prince did with himself; maybe his room was only a door

or two away from where he was holed up with his
limburger, carving soap into cars and boats, getting a
chance to waste the rest of his life in peace because some
monks had decided to honor St. Barnabas by taking care
of bums and cripples. What Gene didn't want to see was
the attendant untying Archie, working the knots loose
and letting him fall forward onto his bed, legs and arms
angled impossibly on the sheet like the chalked outline
of a tenth floor suicide.

"Newfoundland Nat wants to hear from somebody
who's warm." The radio was still on, but Gene didn't
know which switch would send his voice north. "State-
side, this is Nat the Whaler. How hot are you, state-
side?"

Right then Gene decided that Nat was a fraud, that
nobody who hunted whales would underline it, would
use any of these expressions. "Testing," he said into the
microphone, hearing only his unamplified voice. He
tried a black switch and said, "Who are you, really?" into
the microphone, getting nothing again but the low volume of himself. He flipped another switch and said
"Nat, the Whaler, who are you really?"

He knew immediately that he still wasn't sending. He
wasn't even sure, after twenty seconds of Nat's silence, if
the Newfoundland Ham was still on the line, but Gene
knew that Archie wasn't coming back, that his father
was upstairs finishing the limburger ceremony, so he
turned another dial and said "Liar" into the mike, then
"Liar" again as he began to combine switches with dials,
chanting "Liar" while he altered every visible control and
waited to be heard.

Tinderbox

Our routines were as monastic as our lives, writing to girl friends, reading their twice-a-week promises, waiting for weekends to free us from the classes required by our student deferments. The mail was important. What it brought. When it arrived. And Sunday, because there was no delivery, lacked tension and encouraged our small complaints.

After dinner the weekend was finished. Everything loose was piled into trash cans on the back porch of the house we rented from R. C. Blevins, an adjunct physical education instructor at the university. Blevins had started the year with five of us in his renovated poor-side-of-town house, but we'd had casualties, and he checked in with us once a week, following up leads on possible renters, tallying up the income he was losing while he tried to support his family on part-time pay for two sections of Fitness Training.

Blevins was right to be worried. Not one of us was coming back next year, two seniors and myself, a 2-s graduate student. We didn't care whether or not the clutter attracted roaches; the only reason we threw out the garbage was to reclaim enough space in the living room to watch television while we thought about the studying we would eventually get to. True, there was a back and forth procession to the refrigerator, but the late Sunday beers were meant to be sipped slowly, a sort of decompression stage on the way up from the ocean floor of Saturday.

Just a little television, we'd say. Ed Sullivan, or whatever might clear the head. Nothing you watch to think about, except here was Johnson on all the Cincinnati channels one Sunday, having all of us just about convinced to reopen our books with his speech about troop limits and the 20th Parallel as a kind of line in the dirt, drivel so repetitious he might as well have been that talking mouse Sullivan introduced once a month.

Until he said "I will not be a candidate for re-election." Straight out. No Indian-giver clauses. All three of us sat up and leaned forward like we were getting directions for a treasure hunt. McCarthy had shown him the light at the end of the tunnel, all right. New Hampshire had mattered, and each one of us started calculating the reduction in his draft odds, whether or not he had enough slack left in his deferment to maybe ride this one out.

I didn't know about Ken and Bill, what else they could use besides being students, but I knew I was used up on June 30 when I would come up for reclassification. Graduate school didn't carry its weight at the draft board anymore. Not since Tet. I had the call.

I was sending out applications; I suddenly wanted to teach. Even facing nine months of tending juvenile delinquents, if almost having a Master's Degree in American Literature sounded like anything worth being hired for.

We heard Westmoreland quoted: "The enemy has been defeated at every turn," which sounded exactly like the starting gun for retreat. Johnson was looking properly saddened, so nobody wished, like we usually did, for him to go down in front of the country with another coronary.

For a few minutes, in fact, we even felt pretty close to Johnson, had another beer with him while he finished up rationalizing the end of his political career. Then Bill went upstairs to pack for his week on the other side of Ohio observing accountants in Cleveland, and I left Ken to enjoy Sullivan by himself because I had a thesis to defend and a comprehensive oral examination to take on Thursday afternoon. We'd already had two failures at the end of the first semester: one of finances, one of resolve. I had to handle myself better than they had; I needed all three of the months I had left at Miami to work on getting a teaching deferment before the government noticed how big that loophole was.

Ken hadn't received a letter from his girl friend in Syracuse since Tuesday, so maybe he was a little more anxious than I was by Monday at four o'clock. I kept having my preoccupations with lust interrupted by the reading list I was carrying around, memorizing the titles of literary works I hadn't read. It was a pretty skimpy diet of learning I was on, but I didn't feel at all like joining him on the stairs to watch through the glass front door for the black mailman who finished his route with our house because, for all we knew, it was the only one rented to students in this defeated neighborhood Blevins had bought into when he'd decided to become a slumlord.

By quarter to five, when the mailman showed up, Ken had metamorphosized into somebody who showed a compatibility with a wardrobe of sheets and hoods. "We don't want our mail getting here so late," he said, striding out on the porch with the mailman to take what he had for us from his hand.

"We do as well as we can," the mailman said.

"No we don't. We don't do well at all sitting here waiting for our mail until it's almost dark."

The mailman looked like he was sorting through the lines the post office had taught him. He decided on "We're sorry for any inconvenience" and turned to go back down the porch steps.

Ken didn't seem to mind talking to the back of a uniform. "You used to leave mail by two o'clock, and now it's almost five," he said. "We know why it's almost five; we know why you're late." The mailman was back on the sidewalk. "We know where you live," Ken shouted, working himself into a state that could send a man right up beside a flammable cross with a lighter, and when the mailman kept walking, he added "Coon," and then, thinking maybe that his choice of slurs had been too regional, stepped to the edge of the porch and yelled "Nigger!"

I was struck by the mailman's unbroken stride and the collective pronoun Ken had been using for his monologue. "Give it a rest," I said from the doorway. "These aren't the times anymore."

"They never change," Ken said. "The times. Who are you, anyway, the April Fool?"

I saw that neither of the letters were for Ken. For once I didn't care whether or not they were for me. I was getting lightheaded from anticipating my humiliation; I was inhaling nothing but the carbon dioxide of past carelessness.

The next day the message in a bottle came floating in from Mary Soltis, who'd taken her orals Monday evening and sat beside me in my Tuesday afternoon class. I made my point immediately: "Lucky you," I started, "it's all over and done with."

I was unreasonably confident. Mary Soltis was married to scholarship. She was on a full fellowship; she was already enrolled in the Ph.D. program; she was studious and conscientious and what's more, didn't use alcohol or any artificial substitutes. "Lucky you," she said, "who still has his chance. I failed."

All of the early spring heat wave that had rolled into Ohio from the Great Plains was dwarfed by my sudden fever. My pores sagged open like the toothless mouths of the briarhoppers who patrolled the incest country that started south of Oxford and solidified itself in Kentucky.

"The whole thing?" I said, something like investigating the possibility of partial death.

"My thesis was rejected. I failed the comprehensive."

I was seeing the merits of being unschooled. I was seeing why damaged rural children dropped out of junior high school and took to pick-up trucks and shotguns. Certainly it was time to reconsider things over some serious beer, convert myself to a religion that clearly defined its tenets, preferably pacifism. The Quakers seemed select.

"You're doing Faulkner," I said. "How can Faulkner fail?"

"Faulkner wasn't being tested. He didn't have to demonstrate his mastery of the literature of the South."

This was turning into boot camp for the draft, trial by fire for apprehension. "He bounced back," I said. "So will you."

"Who bounced back?"

"Faulkner. His books went out of print during the Second World War and five years later he had the Nobel Prize." Mary Soltis looked as if she had never heard of this. She looked drugged. I was preparing to defend the value of researching Ambrose Bierce, whose only revival in the 20th century had been a story adapted for *The Twilight Zone.*

"I have until August," she said. "I found out you get one second chance and then you're dropped from the program."

Five minutes late, the professor unloaded his briefcase and started right in where he'd left off the week before about the history of the English language. We were up to High and Low German; we were starting to get the picture of what Indo-European meant to all of us on April 2, 1968.

Because I was going to personify a parody of education in forty-eight hours, there was no point in taking notes. I looked over at Mary Soltis, who was busy writing a suicide letter in her notebook. I thought about how shabby it would look after it was yanked out by a policeman. The ragged edge. All of those torn holes. In two days I was going to fail to convince my examination committee why anyone except Rod Serling should give a damn about Ambrose Bierce.

*   *   *   *   *   *   *   *

It proved one thing to me about landlords when R. C. Blevins walked eight blocks over to the house when I called to tell him, Wednesday night, about the swarming termites. Walked quickly. No hesitation. Even with his wife having his car in Hamilton and not expected back for hours. He had an investment.

"How do you know they're termites?" he asked as I led him up the stairs.

"What else could they be?" I answered, emphasizing ignorance through every syllable.

"There are a lot of insects in the world," said Blevins. "You'd be surprised."

I waved my hand toward the closest swarm, the ones that had materialized out of the floorboards of the hallway. "Flying ants," Blevins said, and I agreed they looked exactly like red ants with wings, how I imagined the insect world would adapt after the nuclear holocaust.

"Don't termites do this?" I said. "Don't they have a migratory stage, a few days when they're transformed before settling down to their regular habits?"

Blevins opened the door across the hall from mine, the one I'd slammed shut to keep maybe the dumbest of the winged termites from escaping. For one semester, Lando the Scandinavian, a psychology major, had lived here while he accumulated deficiency points and pounds. He'd gained weight on ready-to-eat snacks, so maybe there was a hygienic reason for the throw rug of termites along one wall. It rose and fell in a way that made me check below my knees to certify that things down there were still intact.

"We have ourselves some flying ants, that's for sure," Blevins said. "Look at them go."

I'd seen enough. I didn't even know what a flying ant was, whether or not Blevins had me figured for such a novice that he was improvising to protect his income.

"It's the weather, for sure," Blevins said. "They've had their alarm clocks rung by the heat."

I thought about Lando failing in that room full of larvae, maybe haunted by some sort of premonition. He'd given me a test that had demonstrated I was mildly schizophrenic. I'd been disappointed and so had he because I hadn't quite come up to snuff as a possible loony.

"You got them in your room? You got a swarm in there about to give you nightmares?" Blevins went ahead and helped himself, but he didn't scare up any ants. I made sure the door was closed when he decided I was clean, that I hadn't drooled sugar on the floor every night I'd lived there. "You going to have to sleep downstairs, that's for sure. One night on the couch won't hurt."

I'd given up on studying for the orals anyway. How could I review the void of my education? I might as well have been walking across Antarctica looking for the barber's pole that marked the center of things.

"I'll go and get something to spray that'll teach these here buggers to show themselves. It's now or never for getting them."

"Where were they yesterday?" I was thinking about the late bloomers under my feet, the Caesarean Section you could do on the walls.

"Who the hell knows?" said Blevins. "They're freaks. There's nothing like this that's natural." He made obscene pumping motions with his right arm. "Couple of shots of the old bug juice. Get 'em while the gettin's good," he finished up, leaving me to move essentials

downstairs, like the victim of a falling sky. Blevins, I was
certain, didn't have any more idea of what he'd just seen
than I did.

"What's the word on the termites?" Ken said, looking
up from the television. He hadn't seen any sign of them
downstairs where his room was; he didn't have any reason to investigate first hand.

"They're incognito." I piled my review books on the
card table we used for meals. *The Penguin Guide to
Victorian Literature* was on top of the stack to discourage
me from getting restarted. "Blevins says they're harmless." I threw my pillow and a blanket on the couch.

Ken nodded. "You don't believe him."

"He's going to spray up there."

"To eradicate the harmless."

"He's taking no chances."

"He should have looked in the mailbox. The
junglebunny didn't take the outgoing mail."

"You ticked him off."

"I sure as hell hope I did."

"He'll get over it. He's got a job to do. He's got government regulations to deal with."

"You're missing the point," Ken said. "I put a banana
in the mailbox for him. I left the son of a bitch a little
something symbolic."

I thought about what to say. "Maybe he didn't understand your meaning. Maybe he didn't even see it."

"He sure as hell saw it. I watched him from the window upstairs in the bathroom. He got all bent out of
shape and threw the mail on the porch, but there was
only a magazine for Bill so it didn't turn out to be much
of a protest or anything."

"We live a half block from the black section. You don't want to be pissing the guy off too much."

"I want him pissed off permanently. I want him to enter a major piss off mood. I want him to see his place in the universe." Ken waved his hand toward the television where an announcer was doing a commentary on the snail's progress of the heavyweight boxing tournament being held to crown a successor to the dethroned Ali. "You know what we need around here, don't you? We need the Great White Hope."

"Ingemar Johansson was a fluke. You saw how hopeless old Lando was."

"That's Swedes. We have enough Swedes. We need Jerry Quarry."

"Nobody needs Jerry Quarry except his wife. Boxing doesn't need Jerry Quarry."

"You're very wrong," Ken said. "It's the times. They're coming back. Quarry'll kick ass on Jimmy Ellis and then he'll kick ass on Joe Frazier who didn't do anything but beat up fatass Buster Mathis who looked like a black Lando flunking out. Everything's in place for Jerry Quarry to shoulder the White Man's Burden."

"What about Ali?" I said.

"Ali's in Muslim heaven. He's out of the picture."

"We're getting out of Nam. He'll be back when it's all blown over."

"Somebody else is getting out of that slime. You and I are about to get in."

"The Slough of Despond," I said, proud.

"Whatever you want to call it, but the body count's way up there in draft-the-graduate land."

After a morning of paralysis, I decided, an hour before my two o'clock orals, to drink a couple of quick glasses of Gallo Vin Rose to get things settled. I went into Lando's old room and tallied the damage Blevins had done to the flying ants. They were dead by the thousands, but I had the feeling they'd traded losses for territory. I knew I was going to be uneasy dropping off to sleep only an average broad jump from where I was standing.

Evidently, the wine was a bad idea. I didn't relax at all, not after walking through Oxford and sweating from my hyperventilated pace. I got to campus without running into anyone, reached Bachelor Hall twenty-five minutes early, and made for the men's room and a series of paper towels. I hung my blazer on a hook; I opened a window and waited for early April to cool me off, but the heat wave that had stirred up the flying ants was still keeping it maddeningly wonderful outside: 75, sunny, a Miami Beach afternoon.

I looked in the mirror, trying to see myself as someone besides a junior high school wiseguy waiting for the principal to slap my ass with the paddle I'd gotten to sign afterwards to show it had all been done in the proper spirit. What had I read in my twenty-two years? All of Tom Swift. The Hardy Boys, Nancy Drew. Marvel Comics. And John Updike.

He was my savior. I knew all about Rabbit Angstrom and what it was like to drive off in a car listening to rock tunes until you turned around and drove back. I knew all about basketball and one time lighting up the hoop for twenty-nine points, seven straight eighteen-footers falling to key a big comeback for a Division III college.

I knew what Updike knew. I could see myself teaching

in a classroom full of oafs who fondled their girl friends while I suffered the arrow in my Centaur's foot. I knew what was inside the opened door, the poorhouse. It was a kind of reincarnation from a life still being lived. I wondered if Updike was bothered by vague apprehensions of ignorance and death, if I could reciprocate.

Professor Chaney, my thesis advisor, saw me step out of the men's room at one fifty-five. "How are you?" he said, leading me into the paneled seminar room without staring at my sweat. The room had everything that made you think something important was going on there, something learned by a select few. Certainly not me. Not somebody who wouldn't be allowed to touch leather-bound books unless he held up his hands to certify they weren't filthy.

"Here is Dr. Palko and Dr. Moss," Chaney went on. "From your other areas of concentration: modern American and modern British."

When we began I gave them a show by talking about Ambrose Bierce. I put on a real tour de force: polarity, disillusionment, insanities and death. I alluded to *Patriotic Gore*; I quoted *The Devil's Dictionary*. I didn't want to leave out anything that would give Palko and Moss a chance to worry through the reading list I'd ignored.

At three o'clock, though, the carillon across the quadrangle rang out something adapted from "Greensleeves" and Moss turned the discussion to D.H. Lawrence and Virginia Woolf, James Joyce and Ford Madox Ford. I held my own with platitudes; I was doing all right until Palko, who'd been staring into the sunshine, said, "What did the thunder say?"

"Pardon me?"

"The thunder. What did it say?" My expression was transformed into the ones taken on by cows when they're asked about the significance of an extra stomach. "Eliot," Palko prodded, and then, seeing me, as I saw myself, standing mournfully behind a fence: "*The Waste Land.*"

"It spoke in a foreign language, didn't it? It blew in from the East."

"In a manner of speaking."

"I don't know."

That seemed to satisfy him, as if he'd been checking up on yet another claim that animals could talk, and now that the fraud had been verified, he could benignly smile.

I didn't go mute, at least. I kept my speech firmly in English until the bells went off again at four o'clock and I had to sit in Chaney's office to wait out the decision. For ten minutes I looked at the dated annual pictures of his family, following his daughters' transformations from larvae into butterflies and making up excuses for my wasted life.

Chaney, when he appeared in the doorway, was beaming. He led me down the hall to handshakes and a sort of welcome-to-the-club exchange of secrets. "You should have asked him to describe the wounds of The Fisher King, Russ," Moss said to Palko, who roared.

I decided to look that one up. It wouldn't hurt to have a sense of literate innuendo now that I knew the requirements of scholarship were stupefyingly low.

I stopped for two six packs. I carried an open quart in my hand for the last six blocks into Oxford's scale model for Selma. Ken was watching a rerun of "The Addams Family" and waiting to see if I was bringing party food.

"Well, how did the sixty-four thousand dollar question work out? You break the bank?"

"Yeah. Isolation booth and all."

"So this isn't for a wake," he said, lifting a can of Schoenling from the package. "Now what?"

"Now I finish the thesis in time and work on my options."

"You have any?"

"Conscientious objector. Canada. Teaching."

"I have a bad knee maybe. I can't see myself as a pacifist. I can't see myself teaching or in the land of the maple leaf."

"All your eggs in one basket."

"One that hasn't been tested, so to speak, for egg weight."

"I know what you mean," I said. "I don't have any track record for religion. I'd starve to death in Canada. I have the bad knee of teaching."

"September, then."

"Do or die."

"Five months to get the old honorable withdrawal into motion."

"The backpedaling."

Ken took a second beer while I watched a former child actor make an ass of himself as a comic vampire. I was hoping the pet hand would rise from its box on the table. "Where's Thing," I said. "Has Thing been in this one yet?"

"I do have some news about another government agency," Ken said.

"Yeah?"

"The post office. It collected the outgoing mail today.

Two bananas. Not to be missed like one. Not to be ignored or sidestepped."

"He left the mail in the box?"

"He performed his duties. He carried off the symbolic
weight of my opinion."

"For evidence."

"For dinner. For when he lets his tail hang out."

I must have let my face go sour because Ken rallied
then: "I don't care if we live alongside jungleland. These
rural spearchuckers never heard of Black Power. They
have the fear: they have these briarhoppers riding herd
on them. I want my damn mail before four o'clock. I
want to hear from my girl friend on Eastern Standard
Time."

"There it is," I said. "There's Thing."

I hadn't gotten any letters. I didn't have anything in
mind except swallowing beer as fast as I could and pretending I'd accomplished something special. An hour
later we were watching an old Perry Mason, betting on
who was guilty, the loser to walk uptown for two more
six packs. The woman Ken had picked was on the stand
getting nervous. It looked like he might have a winner,
but the camera was still panning the courtroom, picking
up the twitches of my suspect.

A CBS News Bulletin came on. "War news," I said,
feeling blessed. "Check this out. The boys are coming
home." Instead, a picture of Martin Luther King appeared behind an announcer who told us he'd been as-
sassinated. Somebody had caught most of it on film,
King on the motel balcony in Memphis, a group of men
pointing with powerless despair.

"Oh shit, man," Ken said. "They're going to be coming out of the walls. They're going to burn down the cities."

The announcer seemed to hear him. "Police in urban areas are on full alert," he said.

"You betcha," Ken said. "You betcha they oughta call out the national guard."

We saw the film twice more. We were promised up-to-the-minute accounts, but Perry Mason didn't return when the broadcast ended. The Cincinnati news team came on to give us the lowdown on unrest in Ohio cities. They said something about Cleveland's Hough District and I thought of Bill, knowing he was nowhere near anything but money. "They going to riot in Syracuse?" I said.

"You betcha."

"What's it called," I said, "the part of Syracuse where the blacks live?"

"Christ, I don't know. Do those places have names?"

"The Hill District," I said, thinking of home, how Pittsburgh would flare up in a couple of places. "Homewood."

"You're a regular encyclopedia."

There was a thump on the wall by the front door. We shut up for a second and there was a second thump. Ken was outside like a kamikaze before I had a chance to check out the window for snipers.

"Goddammit," he said through the doorway. "The goddamn bananas." He held them up like handguns.

"That's probably making him feel better," I said. "That's probably the end of it."

"You're one hell of an encyclopedia."

"We're not the only house on the block. There's plenty of back-up here."

"What we have here," Ken said, "is the white man's burden." He closed the door behind him and a flurry of thumps splattered against the house.

"Bananas," I said. "Think about it." I started to laugh.

"No wonder you're laughing," said Ken. "You don't own anything."

It was true. The television was Ken's. The stereo was Bill's. All of the kitchen appliances belonged to Blevins. Only George, the junior history major who'd run out of money at Christmas, had seemed as tapped out as I was. The only thing he'd sprung for was a couple of bottles of wine when he'd flunked his draft physical because he'd stopped taking his blood pressure medicine.

I could get everything I owned onto the back porch roof in less than five minutes. I could save everything, no doubt about it. Unless they used dynamite, I was in the clear. I didn't have anything I couldn't toss into a cardboard box and throw overboard except my high school graduation typewriter, which was suspect anyway, something I could maybe hit up Blevins for when he filed an insurance claim.

I went upstairs and moved everything to the window.

My father, when he'd dropped me off in September, had looked out that window for a long time. "This is your only way out of here if the place goes up in flames," he'd said. "You won't have a choice of exits in a tinderbox like this."

There was more thumping against the front of the house, but I didn't go back downstairs. I stood in the dark of the bathroom and looked out at a cluster of men on the sidewalk across the street. From time to time, someone would shout, nothing intelligible. I thought it was a code. Nobody could make a series of sounds without occasionally slipping into language.

I went to the top of the stairs and saw that Ken looked out the glass door every time a voice was raised. Everything he did made me vow to keep separated from him, put myself further from harm's way if those voices were a kind of Pavlov's Exam and those were researchers outside, keeping tabs until Ken's face at the door was a verified response. From the bathroom window I could count thirty-four bananas on the porch. No small investment.

Finally, glass broke downstairs and Ken shouted "We're getting into serious difficulty here," which I could suddenly agree with, seeing a fire start up in the front yard, something squat and awkward burning. A grocery bag, probably, filled most likely with gasoline-soaked newspaper or rags. A second one flared, nearer the house by maybe five feet, and then a third, the men who were lighting them putting a fourth bag just a step from the front porch.

It occurred to me when they backed off without tossing a fifth one through the broken window that the sacks were full of old mail, circulars and catalogues—all of them marked Patron or Resident—a lifetime of mail turning into constellations of red stars that winked shut by the time they reached my eye level.

"We've got ourselves a genuine goddamn problem," Ken reminded me, but I was watching a new frenzy in the street. Somebody really crazy was out there now. He was waving a rifle at the dispersing men, bringing technology to this outpost. He was walking on water because nobody was shooting at him from the million shadows, nobody was charging him with the determination of the cornered.

"Goddamned Blevins," Ken shouted up the stairs, and I saw that he was right, that sure enough R. C. Blevins had understood, after an hour of news bulletins, that his property was in no-man's land. And he was the luckiest man alive because already he was slowing down with his shouting and rifle-waving, somehow getting the old fear of the Lord into whoever had bought out the IGA produce section.

"Goddamn!" Ken yelled. "You see old Bwana Blevins out there kicking some ass? You see the goddamn incarnation of the Great White Hope?"

I had to admit it looked like things had settled down. I had to hand it to Blevins. If he didn't get his head blown off in the next couple of minutes, he'd managed to pull it off.

Blevins was milking the moment now. He was standing among the smoldering oversize luminaria, and he was yelling at an empty street. I wanted to go find Eliot; I wanted to bring him back to the window and open it to try a turn at whatever mythology he'd employed. DATTA. DAYA. DHVAM. DAMYATA. Blevins might have appreciated it, a little culture and literacy at a victory time like that, a little class and style, what you get, maybe, from reciting in a foreign tongue.

Grade Nine

I've said some things I wanted to. The summer I moved in with Jack Bittner, for instance. I lost my job at the Heinz plant when I called the foreman exactly what I wanted to.

It made me feel good to get something like that out at least once when it was needed. That day it was 90 degrees all over Pittsburgh. The line was running tomato soup, case after case of the size you buy for your kids at the A&P, and I was keeping after the sealer so nothing got in the way of those cans on their trip to the warehouse.

I was coding, too. Changing the type on the hour so it was the same as what was stamped on the cans. If you look on your can, you'd know your tomato soup came from Pittsburgh and was canned on June 23rd. If you could make out the code. If you cared what those letters and numbers mean.

Some bosses need being crushed, caught by one of the heavy belts and carried down to where they'd be wedged someplace where nothing larger than your hand might fit. This one did. His name was Emil, and he was one of those up-from-the-ranks guys who'd spent thirty years waiting his turn in charge.

"Hey, Carl," he was shouting, "look at the goddamn cans."

It was three o'clock. I was changing the type on the hour, and that was when the sealer decided to miss a beat and stick itself right in the middle of a case of soup, catching it so every case following was backing up and the weight of a dozen of them had buckled up the boxes until a couple had popped out and a few hundred cans were on the floor.

"They're all fucking ruined, Carl," he said. "All these here damned cans shot to hell and you got your head up your ass here."

Emil shut off the line. "You got yourself plenty of clean-up here, Carl," he said, "and now the warehouse is gonna call and say 'Where's the fucking soup?' and I'm gonna say 'I've got a fucking idiot here named Carl Elsiminick who let a million cans fly all over the goddamn factory.'"

I walked down the line and started ripping out the torn cardboard. The cans inside the first carton were all bent to hell, but I didn't care. I'd get the line moving in a minute. The company'd sell the dented stock to us workers at cost and nothing would get lost. Katie, the packer on my line, waved at me. She was glad to get off her feet for a minute or two while I gathered up those cans.

Except Emil wouldn't let it go. "Get the fucking line going," he said. "Get the fucking cans later."

I wasn't going to break my neck walking on a stray can that would flip me as fast as any cartoon banana peel. I kept picking up cans and left one crushed case on the line so there was no starting it up till I was good and ready.

"Hey, Carl, you fucking idiot," Emil started up again.

Which was when I flipped a can at him and said, "You trip on one of these, asshole, and you're maybe fucked up for life."

Emil caught the can. I was surprised, but it didn't matter because he said right away, "You're outta here, Carl. You're through at Heinz."

I went back to the busted case and hauled it off the belt, bumped the ON switch and figured it was just something he'd said. I felt good about saying "asshole" when I was right, but I didn't want outta there.

"You got ears, fuckhead. You're gone." Emil was waving at somebody from security. I stood there watching the cans start coming down the line again, and before ten cases had passed the sealer, I was being escorted out of the plant like one of those guys you see in handcuffs in the paper.

I got some extra money in my last pay, something the union did for you, but there was no getting out of gross insubordination. I was gone and I was looking for a way to save some money, so I moved in with Jack Bittner, a guy who worked Grade Seven because he was so stupid there was nothing they could teach him except errands.

The sealer work was Grade Nine, thirty cents an hour more than Bittner got. Katie the packer got Grade Four because it was still the 1960s and women worked Grade One to Grade Six, not one woman getting as much as Bittner the dufus who just carried samples from one department to another.

"You've got to lighten up some," Bittner said the first night.

"I don't want to."

"Not all the way," Bittner said. "Just some."

"How much is some?"

"Some is some. You decide, but you gotta lighten up some anyway."

I was sitting there in one of the three rooms Bittner rented and wondering how in the hell I was going to get the energy back up to kiss ass again.

We were stuck halfway up a hill above the North Side, which was where the Heinz plant was if you wanted to walk a mile or more to start your shift. Four blocks down from us they were tearing up everything to make way for I-79 when it got here, working its way down from the north. There was a fight going on about a big church, whether or not they should save it. When I got to watching the spires on it instead of answering, Bittner said, "You oughta try bein' a pin boy, you wanna do somethin' with no good to it at all."

I kept looking at that church and wondering who went to it, all of the walking-distance houses gone except for the ones running up this street from the highway. "Nobody's a pin boy anymore," I said.

"When I quit school they had pin boys. You sweated your ass off and some jerk'd toss a ball early and about kill you while his girl friend laughed."

"I took Nikki Rudman bowling once and there was a pin boy. Maybe that was you."

"I don't remember Nikki Rudman," Bittner said. "I don't remember setting up pins for you."

"I never went back. Maybe Nikki Rudman did.

Maybe she went there with some other guy and bowled a 200 game."

"She give you a 200 game?" Bittner said. "Later, you know?"

"No." I didn't want to talk about Nikki Rudman. I didn't want to sleep on Bittner's couch or work ever again where somebody would tell me what to do. Which were bad choices to be considering, since everything pointed right at them going on forever.

Bittner started right in the next day telling me everything that happened at the plant. "I was upstairs in the Power Building," he said, "and there was a guy there in a suit checking all of the stuff out."

"Yeah?" I said. I was drinking Bittner's beer, so I tried listening.

"He was looking in the soup kettles. He was watching the women pulling chickens. You think Heinz fucked up?"

"It's the rabbi," I said.

"Huh?"

"He comes around every once in a while to see if it's kosher."

"What's that mean?" Bittner was looking nervous. He was opening his second Iron City and acting like he realized the next inspection sweep would put him up here on the second floor with me all day.

"Being clean. Stuff like that. Using the right food in the soup."

"Jews send their preacher to check up on what they eat?"

"Yeah. Close enough."

"Jesus."

I opened another Iron. I'd gotten far enough so I wasn't embarrassed pulling tabs on Bittner's beer. A week, I'd said. I'll be out of here in a week. I knew what Bittner was bringing home in his paycheck.

"Nigger down in sterilizing got his hands scalded."

"Yeah? Who's that?"

"Fat one. What's-his-name."

"Blakey?"

"Yeah. Maybe."

"Blakey wouldn't get himself scalded."

"Maybe not, then."

"Blakey's sharp."

"Another fat nigger then. Wasn't wearin' his gloves or somethin'."

"Who'd work sterilizing without gloves?"

"You drink lunch, you drink breaks, you forget your gloves maybe."

I didn't want to argue with Bittner. I concentrated on my Iron and said something about putting my name in at a couple of places.

"You'll show 'em," Bittner said. "Smart guy like you oughta be foreman."

"Yeah," I said. It was hot as hell up under the roof like we were. I wondered how Bittner could stand it every day. My week was two days done. I knew I was going somewhere, so I wasn't going to ask him.

"All them goddamn cans," Bittner said finally. "I wish I'd seen all them goddamn cans backing up that line."

*   *   *   *   *   *   *   *

I spent two or three hours in the morning following up leads from the want ads, but they were all shit jobs—sell-

ing door to door, frying burgers. In the afternoon I
watched game shows, the kind where you can answer
before the contestants. ZAP—I'd push a buzzer on my
knee and say Henry Fonda or Calvin Coolidge or
Chubby Checker, and some guy wearing a navy outfit
would still be stammering around, guessing Chuck
Berry had sung "The Twist" as if he'd never grown up in
America.

The jobs worth having were union. I followed up on
them with phone calls, but the fourth morning I was still
telling Bittner "I've got things to do," and getting my
applicant's outfit together. He was working banker's
shift for a few days, starting at ten so he'd overlap the day
crew by a couple of hours. It was clean-up they'd have
him doing after he was done delivering samples. I'd seen
those guys, usually old and hanging on to retirement,
hosing down spills, pushing broom.

He sort of waved when I left, being casual, but even
Bittner knew I was hustling myself nowhere. I ended up
waiting at the bus stop with an old woman who kept
stepping out to the curb and peering toward the city. I
wasn't that anxious, but she finally got the bus pried
loose from Pittsburgh with her looking, and I rode out
East Street to the McKnight Strip, counting on those
four miles of businesses, the odds with me because
they'd been sucking the life out of the city with conve-
nience for fifteen years.

I tried the Giant Eagle, the Biff Burger, and a chicken
franchise, but I wasn't looking to be a stock boy or a fry
cook. I was asking about assistant manager, the kind of
job where you spend six months getting paid while
you're trained to take over a new place opening ten miles

up the road. Things were getting crowded out here, they kept saying; a lot of smart kids were having to work counters until things opened up again.

I didn't have that kind of time. I checked out two car dealers and I filled out papers, but I could see three or four guys in each place drinking Cokes and smoking while they watched the lot for somebody who might turn into a commission.

Finally I crossed over to where they were renovating an old shopping center, putting a roof over it so they could compete with the mall at the other end of the strip. I figured this place might be hopping in a few months, that the stores would be gearing up for the boom the remodeling was going to bring.

Nothing. I couldn't get a handle on why the place wasn't full of openings, and after a dozen visits with secretaries, I talked with the mall's manager, who told me I could work security if I gave him forty-eight hours to check me out and I was willing to work nights.

"It's a promise," he said after we talked. "Next Monday, three o'clock. If you don't hear from us before then, you've got a place."

I'd never heard it like that before, so I knew it was going to be a shit job, something Bittner could do. It paid like Grade One—it paid like I was one of those old women who sat on a stool all day sifting through dried vegetables on a conveyor belt, lifting out odd pieces, stems, whatever they were supposed to be checking for.

It was a start, something to fall back on. I retraced the length of the mall-to-be, feeling how the main aisle had a ridge running along it, as if they hadn't matched the

seams quite right when they'd sewn those stores together. It made me wonder about who was foreman
here, where he'd been when this flaw was turning permanent. I hiked up the highway another half mile, one
more car dealer, a Long John Silver.

Eventually I got to a restaurant with a bar, so I decided
to take a break. It was like a movie theater inside, dark
enough I had to stand there for ten seconds making sure
there wasn't a step to fall down. I ordered a cheeseburger
and a draft, getting two refills before the burger showed
up. I noticed two guys in suits sitting in a booth, but
other than them there was only a woman who was wearing a Century 21 blazer. I kept looking her way, and
when she smiled I took my fourth beer over to where she
was sitting.

"How are houses going these days?" I said.

"South," she said.

"I know what you mean."

"I bet you sell cars," she said, finishing her drink.
"Something foreign."

"Not many cars getting sold today," I said.
"Everything's slowing down but the army."

"Good time for serious drinking." She waved her glass
and got another Screwdriver. I chased down my beer and
waited for her to confess how bored she was, how she
wanted to get out of that gold jacket and relax. She was
maybe thirty-five; she had enough left of her body to
make me want to drink beer until something happened.

"You know something," she said, and I perked up. "I
haven't made one nickel selling houses for six weeks." I
didn't know what she wanted to hear from me; I figured
my silence would let her get on with it, how she didn't

care anymore and just wanted to get drunk and in bed with somebody to forget bad times for a while. "Six weeks," she went on, "you don't sell a car for six weeks and you're gone, right?"

"Right," I said, automatic, keeping her going in my direction.

"I still got this damn coat. I still got couples with two babies standing in kitchens trying to sort out how they could ever keep up payments with the wife at home changing diapers all day." She polished off her drink and seemed to be thinking about what came next.

"You know the last thing I sold?" she said.

"No clue," I answered.

"A garage." She held the glass in front of her eyes as if she were checking for scratches. "A shitty little two-car garage for six thousand dollars. You know what the commission is on six thousand dollars? You look smart enough; you can guess."

"Why don't we get out of here?" I said, trying to hurry things a little.

"I ask myself that every day," she said.

I got up. "You ask it today yet?"

"Yeah."

"And?" I stood there running out of time from being so obvious.

"I said to myself, 'There's still something here. Somebody knows that because they're going to build a new mall right across, practically, from the old one.'"

I was standing there listening to the last lines I was ever going to hear from this woman, but I swirled the end of my beer to buy time. "They're four miles apart," I said. "It's just a renovation."

She sat up then and stared at me. "You don't sell Triumphs," she said. "You don't sell anything around here." I swallowed the beer. "Christ," she said, "everybody knows they're going to break ground for a brand new mall right up the street."

"What for?" I said.

"Who the hell knows?" she said, "but all the big stores will be moving in there when they open in two years." I put the glass down, but she didn't make any move to get up. "What the hell *do* you do?" she said.

"I work in the city," I said. "Marketing."

"Sure," she said. "You're a hell of a salesman, aren't you?" She waved her glass again. "See you around sometime. Maybe I can sell you a house if you move out this way."

"After the babies come," I said, and at least she laughed.

The fifth day I rode the bus into Pittsburgh. I thought I'd try the department stores. I worked my way from Hornes to Gimbels to Kaufmans, trying to understand every step of the way how those guys selling blenders could afford the suits they were wearing. Heinz had been paying me a dollar an hour more; Bittner's Grade Seven got 70 cents an hour more.

I finally said what-the-hell and yanked off my tie on the way down Liberty Avenue. I shoved it in my pocket and took off my coat and carried it like a lunch pail. Down at the end of Liberty by the Hilton Hotel, the Three Rivers Arts Festival was going on, and even this early on Friday there were enough people sweating in the sun to make you wonder why artists didn't all get rich.

I trudged around for a while, looking at the three-dimensional stuff, a big graffiti-covered canvas tunnel that looked like a vacuum cleaner tube. I wanted to write "What the fuck?" on it, but it seemed like the guy who'd built it had picked up on anti-war slogans. PEACE WORM it said on a sign. Underneath the name it said NOT FOR SALE.

I climbed on a bunch of steps that were really longer and longer poles sawed off into stumps. The sign there said PLEASE EXPLORE ME and STAR CLIMB. A bunch of kids were hopping from one stump to another, and I started feeling tall and stupid, so I got myself down from there and went over to the river, the Allegheny side where a wire was rigged up from the bank to the bridge, stretching maybe two hundred feet and looking scary enough to keep a big crowd around waiting to see what was going on.

Richard Reeves, The Rocket Cyclist, was hunched over the handlebars of a revving motorcycle. I wanted to see this. I worked my way up to the front row, standing almost under the wire Reeves would ride on his way to the bridge.

Reeves took off right after I got into position, and the first thing I noticed was how the wheels were locked onto the cable, how there was no way for this rocket cyclist to kill himself unless he decided to simply let go of everything. A guy next to me shouted "Bullshit" and after Reeves started doing loops around the cable so even a six year-old could tell there was no danger, I knew it was time to get back to Bittner's and start on his beer.

I decided to hike back up the Monongahela side, looping around the point where some trick high-divers were entertaining the crowd that hadn't fallen for Richard Reeves. A hundred yards up the river there was a guy flying something like a hang glider with an engine attached. He was actually flapping the wings, and I wanted to wave him on down closer to the crowd since hardly anybody seemed to be watching. He just kept circling. I got the feeling this guy wasn't on the schedule, that he was just horsing around the way somebody throwing Frisbee might show off hoping he'd catch one behind his back just when some beautiful girl was walking by.

So there I was heading as slow as I could along the Monongahela side toward a bus to Bittner's, and the wings simply folded into a tight V. I watched this guy stall like one of those cartoon animals who've run off the edge of a cliff and do just fine running on air until they realize where they are and then shoot down to some bullseye painted on the canyon floor.

It didn't look like Richard Reeves out there on the river when the winged man hit the water. He started struggling right away, and I realized that as soon as those wings took on enough water to sink, he was out of luck unless he could unload himself from the harness.

I knew I couldn't swim. I knew the dozen or so people fascinated by this guy thrashing were making no moves at all toward rescue. Maybe a minute went by, nearly all the time the birdman had, and then a boat showed up, what looked like two guys out drinking on the river who must have thought they were hallucinating that motorized hawk.

It took them a while to haul the flyer into the boat. Those wings were pretty clumsy to handle, and the men in the boat had been drinking beer in the sun. When it was all taken care of, I made a last check of the territory: I was practically alone; the divers were still flinging themselves off the board two or three at a time; the boat full of wings was traveling upriver and probably not even making the news.

After that, I didn't get on the bus. I wasn't ready for Bittner's couch yet, so I walked up Liberty past a half dozen surplus stores where the windows were full of camouflage shirts and hunting knives. I walked past the Art Cinema where the tit movies were pulling in nobody but kids and old men, and then I cut to my left and took the next bridge to the North Side, committing myself to slogging the whole way up River Avenue.

Which meant I had to go by Heinz, why I was walking maybe, because I ended up standing on the corner where the parking lot stopped and the factory pushed almost down to the river. I didn't know if there was a name for the building I was standing in front of, but I knew what was happening in there, some stooge like me hoisting hundred pound sacks of flour and dumping them into a bin whenever the signal came from the floor below. It wasn't a bad job except for the dust and the way the threads sometimes snagged when you yanked them to open the bag.

I walked past vinegar and knew somebody was suffering in there. I passed the warehouse and the research building, the best place I ever worked because you didn't follow a production line. Instead, you waited for some college pro to fool around with the recipe for ketchup. You opened a couple of valves for him whenever he decided it was time, and wondered what difference it would make to anybody's meat loaf if you hesitated five seconds.

What I was sure of was that nobody was working in there. Bittner carried samples all through those halls, staying in the air conditioning as long as he could with those six packs of tomato sauce.

And then there was nothing left to River Avenue but old warehouses and garages, places where winos parked themselves. I was tired as hell. I turned left again and made my way back across Federal Street and up toward Bittner's apartment, another two miles before I could start to wash away the furnace hike.

"I can get on with Rent-A-Cop at the Gimbel's shopping center, the one they're fixing up out there," I told Bittner after he got home from his shift. "I'll be out of here as soon as I find a place closer. I got all weekend to look."

"No problem," Bittner said. I wondered if he ever brought a woman up here, how sweaty you could get humping somebody in June when the inversions took over the city.

"You oughta get a fan or something," I said.

"I oughta get a lot of things. I oughta get so much beer in me I'd float right off this fucking hill."

I told Bittner about the guy who'd fallen into the Monongahela. "Like Icarus," I added at the end, but Bittner didn't seem to notice. Probably I was a jerk for even bringing it up, something you had to read in order to know, but for a second I thought a story like that would interest Bittner who ended up just sitting there looking like he thought I'd said something like "Up your ass,"

slurring it real quick so you could back off if somebody
called you on it.

I waited for him to say something, then, because I
wasn't volunteering the story of my walking for miles
through the ass-end of Pittsburgh and standing like
some would-be scab outside the plant. He got up for
another beer. He switched on the TV and then forgot
about it, facing me instead. I started guessing this was
when Bittner would finally tell me my time was up and
to get the fuck out of there.

It turned out he was working up to telling me about
Emil getting his arm ripped off in the sealer. Bittner
wasn't much with detail, so the story was short. "Guy
told me Emil was all pissed off about something stuck in
there," Bittner said. "Emil got to jerking it around and it
finished its cycle. Whop! Just like that, his arm pinned
and then yanked forward so it smeared all over, and the
whole floor got filled up with Emil screaming."

Bittner sat there checking me out for a reaction. I
thought maybe he was making it up, that you wouldn't
lose more than a hand or some fingers in a sealer. "His
whole arm?" I said.

"Fucking-A. Institution-size line. Emil picked the
wrong goddamned sealer to fuck up on."

"Shit," I said.

"Goddamn serves him right," Bittner said, "pissant so
hyper all the damn time for nothin.'"

"He did get hyper, that's for sure," I said.

"For sure he's got nothin' comin' outta his sleeve. For
sure he's gonna be messin' with no more sealers."

Bittner wanted me to do some gloating. He lowered
his beer right down in a couple of swallows and opened

one for both of us. You'd think that Emil would have remembered about the cycle finishing when you cleared the machine. Even Bittner working Grade Seven would remember something like that. You'd think I'd be as satisfied as Bittner wanted me to be hearing that Emil went down the fucking tubes like I'd wished on him, but I didn't say anything else.

I was thinking about another chance at Heinz, how I might work it out with Emil out of the action. I'd put in a couple of years on those sealers; I knew what was going on in that department, and Emil sure as hell wasn't coming back tomorrow to set things straight.

I could grovel a little; the union could make a case if it thought there was a shot at success. I just had to explain things, act like I was wrong about everything and knew sealers enough to be worth bending my case.

That's how I'd sell it, I thought, turning toward the television that was on behind Bittner. Emil had other things to worry about; he didn't have to save any face with an empty sleeve to carry around. I saw that Bittner's TV was tuned in to "Gunsmoke", one of those shows that had lasted me right up from junior high school, and I wanted to see how it came out, whether Doc was going to get himself killed saving the marshal. You might have seen that one. Everything turned out. I don't remember how, exactly, but I remember that much.

Six Letters, Starting With E

There were two men on the roof. Sidway thought they were putting on shingles, but they looked like they were doing something else as well, seeding the roof to guarantee some later destruction, some need for repair they would charge exorbitantly for.

They talked loudly and laughed a lot. As if they had been in a bar all morning, as if they'd been drinking on the job. "It gets hot up there, I imagine," Sidway said to one of them when he approached the edge and searched the ground around him for something Sidway couldn't see.

"Not that hot," the man said. He was skinny and wore a khaki T-shirt that flapped at the arm holes. Sidway thought he might have been in the army once, might have worn that shirt when he weighed forty more pounds. He thought of the pictures of Rock Hudson that had been in the paper all summer because this roofer's face looked like AIDS had been sucking it in for months.

"It's hot enough down here," he said.

"That don't matter none. It ain't that hot up here 'cause we don't work roofs if'n it gets hot." The man on

the roof acted like he'd spotted what he'd walked over
for and was satisfied; he turned and made his way back to
his partner, and almost immediately Sidway heard them
laughing again. He imagined them saying "Hot enough
for you?" and thinking it was hilarious.

As soon as they stopped laughing he heard something
clattering across the roof. He looked up and spotted a
bucket tumbling over the edge. He backed up a step, but
it landed ten feet away, half-heartedly splattering tar-
like drops of paste. Nobody on the roof laughed.

Sidway found Welke, the contractor, in the basement.
"Moving right along, isn't it?" he said to get something
started.

"It's moving along," Welke agreed. "It's always moving along, I hope."

Sidway laughed, but Welke looked like he was just
waiting out the next line, why Sidway had shown up, his
complaint maybe, a stupid question. "Looks good so
far," Sidway said.

"That's what we're paid for," Welke said. He was almost as thin as the man on the roof. "Excuse me," he
said, "got to get to this," and he waved a scroll of draw-
ings that Sidway thought he'd probably agreed to
months before, nodding at the dining room table so
Welke would leave a few minutes earlier. What careless
mistakes had already been made? What foolishness were
the workmen laughing about as they drank beer on his
roof?

*   *   *   *   *   *   *   *

At the end of November, Sidway took a vacation day,
starting to paint on a Friday morning because he could

never finish in one weekend. He was saving himself over a thousand dollars. He was looking for hairline cracks in the floor and the ceiling that would spread and yawn open a week after his family moved in. He was gauging how far from plumb the walls were, how uneven they were, rippling under the paint roller. ONE COAT, the paint can had printed on its label, but Sidway wasn't that naive.

When nobody else showed up all morning, he calculated another delay. It was deer-hunting season, the men refusing to work, so by the time a truck parked out front in the early afternoon, unmarked like the generic brand for hauling, Sidway was half-surprised.

He watched a short, muscular black man get out of the truck and then went back to his wall, relieved he wasn't doing a ceiling, something where he'd be stretched out awkwardly so anybody could tell he didn't have the right tools or the sense to adjust somehow. He rolled on one strip of paint and the man was beside him, startling Sidway because there was no way anyone from the truck could have come around to the side door that quickly.

Sidway hadn't anticipated anyone marching right up the narrow board to the front door. Who would choose to tightrope across the deep ditch left around the house for a reason he didn't know? Only the side door, where the garage was being finished, had access that wasn't threatening. This morning he'd had his son open the front door for him, before he'd dropped him off at the elementary school, the key Welke had given Sidway only good for one lock. Aaron had walked up the board with no trouble, but this truck driver must have practically run up it to get inside so quickly.

"Cabinets," the man said. Sidway wondered where the truck was from; there was only one black family in the whole county, and the father was a schoolteacher.

"Guess you'll have to bring them around through the side door," he said.

"Nobody here?"

"Just me."

"Nobody here," the driver said again. "Nobody working today?"

"Just us amateurs."

"You got a minute to give me a hand?"

Sidway thought there had to be a second man on the crew, but he put the roller down and followed the driver to the side door. The kitchen was already full of heating units and door frames.

"Somebody else already took the easy way," Sidway said. The heating unit boxes were stacked only a few feet from the door. "There's a back door downstairs," he added.

The black man looked out the rear of the house through the ceiling-high window, but Sidway could tell he wasn't considering the back door as a choice. He was evaluating the size of the window, who would pay for something like that.

"Front door's no good either," Sidway finally said. "That board's pretty tricky." He thought of his eight year-old balanced over the ditch, and the driver hoisted a door frame, carried it to the front wall and leaned it against where Sidway had painted during the morning. "Maybe the paint's dry already," Sidway said. "It looks like it might be." The driver was already carrying a sec-

ond door, the stapled-on frame flopping around where
he didn't support it.

"I'll give you a hand. It'll go faster." Sidway picked up
a door frame, handling it carefully so it wouldn't get
marked, so it wouldn't mar the fresh paint. There was no
place to stand it except against the wall.

"Paint looks good," the driver said. "You get the second coat on there and you're ready to get these here cabinets hung up all over the damn place."

They got an aisle cleared to the side door and went
outside. A fine drizzle was misting. "You got to move
that car of yours," the driver said, so Sidway backed up a
little, wondering how many steps would be saved. The
driver waved him back some more and then stepped up
into the truck cab, backing the truck over the low curb
where the driveway would be, spinning through the mud
until he stopped inside the cement-blocked garage area.

"Can't be draggin' no cabinets from out there," he said
when Sidway paused to stare at the tire track furrows.
"Here we go now. Let's get this done."

Sidway called Welke Friday night to complain. There
were still two boxes sitting outside. "Rain won't hurt
them," the driver had said. "We got no more room until
somebody takes care of them furnaces." Welke's wife's
voice answered, telling Sidway to leave a message, but he
hung up. He wasn't going to lose the drama of those tire
furrows and ruined cabinets by spilling it to an answering machine.

It rained on and off all weekend. Sidway painted four
bedrooms and hoped the hunters would get pneumonia;
he painted three bathrooms and hoped they would shoot
each other in the fog that settled in on Saturday. By the

time he was working on the basement rec room, he knew
there was no way he could do more than one coat until
after the house was done, until after the carpets were laid
and there were things to ruin.

He noticed the ringing in his ears on Monday morning. All day he listened to it, and after the news ended,
he started reading to his wife: "Tinnitus," he said, "a
constant ringing in the ears caused by a disorder of the
auditory nerve. It may or may not go away."

"Listen to this," he said to his wife. "Listen to what
I've got now. Can you believe it? From out of nowhere.
From painting the house."

"You didn't get anything from painting but a headache."

"I never had tinnitus until I painted for three straight
days. All those narrow closets. All that bad ventilation. I
had all the windows shut; that's as good as a smoking
gun."

His wife turned back to her crossword puzzle. She
said, "That's for presidents, Will; that's for catching
Nixon or somebody like that," and then she started
working on the corner that began with ninety-seven
Down.

"There's more diseases than there are stars, Lois; I
swear it. I used to feel sorry for trees because all those
bugs could get at them, or all those funguses, or somebody could just come along and kill them anyway they
wanted to." He looked over at the puzzle, saw she had a
corner at the top that still had a lot of white. Sooner or
later she was going to have to ask him some words. "But
now," he kept on, "now I've found out people get more
diseases than anything in the universe. We've got too

many parts; we're too complex. We even get things that
nothing else is affected by. Tinnitus. You think the dog
has to worry about being driven mad by tinnitus? We
have to worry about rabies. We have to worry about
tapeworms."

Lois was on the last corner she hadn't worked, and
nothing was helping her connect to where the blanks
were. "It's like hearing a dog whistle twenty-four hours a
day," Sidway said. "That's what it's like. It's maddening.
I wish the hell the dog would hear it; she'd probably like
it. She'd probably hear music in it somewhere."

His wife erased a word. "Give up yet?" he said.

"They're going to make me quit one of these days," she
said. "A local paper and they think they're the *New York
Times* or something."

"Try one out on me."

"Auricular, ten letters starting with S."

"Senescence."

"You look these up before I do them."

"I knew senescence. I know all about it."

"Philosopher d'Abano, six letters; I don't know what it
starts with."

"Pietro."

"Musical movement, six letters, starting with E."

Sidway thought for a moment, buying time, but he
knew immediately that he was stumped. He didn't know
anything about music; he couldn't even answer the easy
Jeopardy questions in that category. "You sure?" he said.
"You sure that's the right number of letters?"

"I can count to six, Will."

"What else is filled in?"

"An R, another E."

"Maybe you have something wrong running through it."

"The other words fit. One of them is your 'senescence.'"

"It can't be impossible. Think of who does these puzzles; think of who lives around here."

"You're stumped."

"It's the ringing in my ears. I can't concentrate."

"We got a bill today that'll make your ears ring louder," Lois said. "We got a bill for one hundred thirty-one dollars for heat."

"It's the time of year."

"It's for the new house."

"Nothing's hooked up in there. The computer went crazy somewhere."

"Something's hooked up. Six or seven baseboard units."

Sidway listened to the dog whistle in his head, but nothing was coming. "The computer went crazy," he repeated. "You can't end up paying one hundred thirty-one dollars for a few units set at 55 degrees."

"The door was left open one weekend. You don't know what the workmen set the thermostats at while they're in there."

Sidway had never heard his wife say anything about heat. "Unlocked?" he said.

"Open. Wide open. I told you about it."

"I thought you meant unlocked." He didn't remember her telling him anything at all.

"It was cold. I saw it open on a Sunday afternoon when I took the boys for a ride to see how things were going."

"Isn't the contractor responsible?"

"I don't think so."

"Welke should pay."

"Welke said he was sorry."

"You told him and that's all he said?"

"I told him and at least he heard me."

"One hundred thirty-one dollars for heat for a house we don't even live in. That's a stumper all right. That's worse than 'musical movement, six letters starting with E.'"

His wife looked at him. "You pay attention when I mention money," she said. "You don't hear the rest of it."

"Might as well work on the rest of the puzzle," Sidway said. "Might as well get something done while my paycheck blows out the front door. Maybe we can work around 'musical movement.'"

Sidway was tired of his new house already, tired of dry wall and beading, words he had learned in the last few weeks and had never seen in a crossword puzzle. Eight letters, starting with T, he said to himself, a curse on homebuilders, but he knew Lois was right about his not listening. He certainly hadn't been listening six months ago when they'd agreed to paint the whole interior, thirty hours of it as things turned out, and this ringing in his ears. And there were baseboards to stain and varnish. And doors. He hadn't even thought of doors as something to finish, but there were fifteen of them standing in his half-done kitchen. Sidway had thought they came with the walls, had begun to see himself as foolish as someone who believed food automatically came in containers, someone who ate a TV dinner raw, somebody who would ask which part of a cow pepperoni came from.

His current neighbors all looked like the workmen Welke hired. That was one reason why he was moving. They wore t-shirts when it was warm, or when it was cold, t-shirts that stuck out at the open throat of flannel shirts, and though Sidway didn't know why, they all ignored or hated him.

They were probably right to, he thought, and right to be happy at his FOR SALE sign. His neighbor from across the street drove a tractor trailer that he parked right in front of his house, standing the trailer on supports and keeping the cab separate while he was off the road, overhauling the engine or washing the cab between each trip.

"We're not getting our price for the house because of that truck," Lois had been saying for two months.

"What's he fix every week?" Sidway kept saying, watching his neighbor lean into the motor with tools he didn't recognize.

"Maybe it'll break in Montana or some place where they still use horses," Lois would say.

Once, Sidway had seen his neighbor raise his leg and deliver a kick to the side of the cab, driving his heel into the door. From where he was standing, Sidway hadn't been able to tell if there was a dent or not, but his neighbor had pulled a handkerchief from his back pocket, had begun to rub carefully at the spot he had struck, moving one hand over it slowly as if tracing a scar.

The ringing in his ears stayed with Sidway all week, and by the time he got through to Welke, the cabinet boxes were inside, the furrows doubled by another delivery truck.

"We lost a man today," Welke said after he'd reassured Sidway.

"Somebody quit?"

"He went down."

Sidway didn't want to volunteer another question that would show his ignorance. He just said "Oh?"

"Off the board," Welke said at last. "Just like that. Never saw anything like it." Sidway listened to the voice spiraling at him through the line, imagined the words about paralysis or death forming twenty miles away. Like a nova, reaching his ears so long after they'd been spoken nothing could make any difference, not sympathy, not surprise. "Busted his back is what he did," Welke went on. "Delbert Zone. All he was doing was door frames and baseboards. Delbert Zone's been doing baseboards for twenty years. Can you imagine how many boards he's walked and today he takes himself a tumble on one of my jobs and breaks his back."

"Hurt bad?" Sidway finally tried.

"He's still got his legs, if that's what you mean. He'll walk again."

"That's good."

"Good for Delbert Zone, but not good for us. We've got ourselves another delay."

"That's ok," Sidway said, though as soon as he let it out, he was enraged.

"I have to make some calls. See if anybody's free to finish up Zone's work."

"I understand."

"Old Delbert Zone's going to be in a body cast. He's not going to be doing any bending for a while."

"It'll get done, right?" Sidway said. He heard the ringing in his ears as if the sound was coming from Welke's end of the line. It could have been Welke testing something; it could have been CONELRAD at a higher pitch.

"He's lucky as hell, really," Welke said. "You don't break your back too often and walk afterwards. It's a nasty fall off a board like that, tools and stuff being carried."

"You never had that happen before?"

"Never. Never even heard of it before."

"My son. My older son goes up that board."

"He's in no danger."

"He opens the door for us with the key. He thinks it's a big deal."

"Once in a lifetime," Welke said. "It's passed now."

"I do it because you're scared," Aaron said to Sidway when he hung up the phone. Sidway hadn't noticed him listening; he cursed the doorless kitchen again, another reason why he was moving.

"I thought you liked going up and down the board. I thought you wanted to."

"I do, but I didn't know you could fall off."

"Donkey ears."

"Who fell off? Is he dead?"

"A guy named Delbert Zone, and he's not dead. He's not even badly hurt."

"He hurt something. What'd he hurt?"

"His back. He broke his back."

"What happens when you break your back? Mom has a student who broke her back falling off the school bleachers, and she's in a wheelchair forever."

"Not every time," Sidway said. "You don't get hurt bad every time."

"She can't ever walk again. She sued the school and they have to pay her money for the rest of her life."

"Delbert Zone's going to walk again."

"How come, if he broke his back?"

"I told you," Sidway said. "It doesn't always happen."

"What?"

"Paralysis. You can break your back sometimes and not be paralyzed."

"I didn't think you could fall off."

"I didn't think so either."

"But you're afraid to walk up it. You never walked up it yet."

"I thought you liked to."

Lois walked in. Sidway imagined she'd been listening until the reruns had started and was coming in now to switch channels. "It's just an accident," she said to Aaron, who was still stuck right beside the phone as if it were going to ring again and bring a medical update on Delbert Zone. "If you're careful," Lois said, "accidents don't happen twice."

"I'm not careful," Aaron said. "I shut my eyes sometimes and pretend I'm blind when I walk the board. I pretend it's a thousand miles down instead of ten feet."

"Just keep them open from now on. Just be careful now."

"I didn't know you could fall off," Aaron said. He kept on standing beside the phone. The ringing Sidway heard was a million miles away.

Saturday morning Sidway drove the two miles to his new neighborhood, bringing just Aaron with him. "It's no problem, you'll see," Sidway said four times while they crossed town, but Aaron wasn't talking. He didn't say anything when Sidway handed him the key. He didn't even look up, but he covered the distance to the board, slipping a little in the mud that reappeared as soon as the sun touched the early December frost. The key, Sidway noticed, was wrapped in his fist instead of being ready between his fingers.

Aaron stepped onto the board, but as soon as both feet were off the ground, he got stuck. "It's all right," Sidway said, coming up behind him. "It's the same board you've walked up fifty times already."

"No, it isn't," Aaron said.

"It's the same. Look, it has spots in the same places."

"It's not the same. It's shakier; it's crooked; it's going to fall as soon as I get in the middle." Aaron backed off. "You go up; you said you weren't scared," he said, shoving the key at him.

"You've got to do it," Sidway said.

"Let Jason do it. Go get him. He doesn't know you can fall off."

"Jason's only five. He's not big enough."

"You're as scared as Jason."

"You won't learn anything this way," Sidway said. "Here, we'll straighten this thing out a little so it doesn't wobble as much." He moved the board a few inches; he was sure it looked like the same trip to Aaron. "Ok, now let's give it a try. You want to hold onto me for the first step?"

Aaron got on the board again and took Sidway's hand. "Now we're going," Sidway said. "Now we've got it." Aaron was inching forward, not picking up his feet. It took him a minute to get far enough that Sidway would have to let go of his hand soon. "Slow but sure," he said. "It doesn't matter how fast. Now all you have to do is take one step and you've got the door knob in your hand."

"Don't let go, Dad," Aaron said.

"I've got to. You can't reach from there."

"I'll fall."

"One step. You could take one step if you were on a string."

"Don't let go."

Sidway pulled his hand away and Aaron froze, crouched, his hands thrown out to the side. "See?" Sidway said. "You're still up there. You're Ok."

"If I move, I'll fall."

"Then you're stuck there forever. They'll finish the house and fill in the ditch and you'll be stuck there like that, standing like a statue on a board that's lying on the ground." He saw Aaron's foot slide backwards an inch, two inches. He shut up then and backed away, looking down the street and across the intersection to the abandoned barn, the last bare sixty acres for a mile in any direction. The sign dangling from the side said FOR SALE—COMMERCIAL. Sidway had read that notice a hundred times and never heard its message. Now he saw a rash of trailers breaking out, an industrial park specializing in noxious fumes. "It'll never sell commercial," the real estate agent had said. "It's been on the market for two years. There's no potential here."

He saw a sprawling government-subsidized housing project, the barracks-like buildings, the junked cars, the broken swings and swarms of children, all of them preschool and wanting to play with his son Jason when they were locked outside by their desperate parents. It would sell on Monday. He noticed a car slowing as it went by, someone estimating how many illegal immigrants would fit on the land.

Aaron poked the key into his side. "You do it," he said, and he trudged back through the mud to the car.

How wobbly could a board be? Sidway thought. Construction workers carried things and walked these. They logged a hundred thousand trips on boards like this one, sometimes with snow crusted on the surface, and he'd never heard of anybody falling except Delbert Zone.

Sidway estimated the distance he'd have to cover when he was committed and vulnerable. Two or three short steps. The cabinet man must have bounced half way up and opened the front door before his other foot had touched down. Like making a routine lay-up, getting the shot off before being called for traveling. You really could do it on a string if your first step was sound. Aaron, he thought, might have his head down, waiting for him to shout from the doorway or as he tumbled into the ditch, but he couldn't take the chance of looking the fool: once he got on the board there was no question about stopping or inching along.

Three steps, he said to himself, and positioned his feet on the board. Immediately, it tilted and wobbled, and Sidway saw that it was too narrow, that if Welke had been careless here, the house would be full of cut corners. He saw that if he didn't get to his front door, things would begin to break even as they unpacked.

Three steps. The ringing in his ears was suited to the rhythm of it, flat and toneless. He looked down into the moat like you weren't supposed to, but it was impossible to do anything else. His ears hammered out their tune. He pushed off: one, two, three, and he was tettering half way up the board, his steps so short he'd used them all and only killed himself by reaching an unbalanced point of no return. Four, five, six, seven, and he lunged for the doorknob, trying not to kneel and clutch it with both hands.

Sidway jabbed the key at the lock, but it wouldn't go in. For a moment he felt it begin to slide from his fingers, but he reversed it and the key lost itself in the lock, turning the handle with almost no pressure.

Sidway stepped into his house and pivoted in the doorway. He was going to shout at Aaron, who was tossing stones, trying to reach the stop sign that was fifty feet further than he could raise, but instead Sidway looked across the street at his neighbor's windows, trying to see if there was movement behind any, somebody who'd been watching and thinking about quitting his job and buying a tractor trailer. Upstairs, Sidway thought, there was something that might give away a sentinel. He stared, waiting for the shadow to recede. He'd give it a minute if he had to. He had the time.

The Man Who Played
For The Skyliners

Fetler nudged the wheel and pulled into the passing lane, pushing the Volkswagen bug up toward sixty-five where it shuddered as if it understood the speed limit signs. He was on one of those straight four-lane highways designed to be driven at seventy, and even though the truck was rolling at a good clip, he knew there was a long grade coming up and the Volkswagen could use a running start.

He was alongside the truck's rear wheels when it swerved left. Fetler jammed the brake pedal down, the Volkswagen locked up into a four-wheel drift, and he was over the median into the oncoming lanes before he could lift his foot. He got traction as his foot came up, and though the car lurched and nearly rolled, he was able to jerk the wheel enough to keep the car from spinning. Instead, it righted itself, heaving, and faced back toward the median while Fetler, seeing that the highway was blank, fired across the divider a couple of hundred yards behind the truck and the compact car it had passed.

Untouched. Fetler said it to himself as he settled the Volkswagen at fifty and waited for his heart to slow.

There was another hour's drive in front of him. The approaching traffic was routinely heavy, and yet he had flown right into the eye of it. The truck and the compact, even on the grade, were pulling away. A dozen cars passed him within the next mile. He wondered which of the drivers had witnessed the miracle. Fetler was closing in on Pittsburgh, following Route 22 across the state. It was not quite noon; his uncle's funeral was at two.

Untouched. He smiled five miles later, Johnstown behind him, and thought of the seasonal way most deaths came, bunched together in generational bundles. All of the funerals he had attended had come before he was fifteen and after he was thirty-five. His family died in clusters, falling aside at sixty-six, sixty-eight, an occasional seventy, all of them knowing it was the heart that would drop them—blood pressure, rich food, unnecessary weight—everyone over forty had that ruddy complexion that looked like health. It was the German curse; it was gravy and potatoes and red meat and sausage and beer on tap in the basement.

"We're quick with our dying," his mother had said at his father's funeral the November before. "It's best. No cancer. No extended pain." Fetler was turning forty this year. Ever since his father's death he had been waking up in the night convinced he was dying, sweat squeezing out of him as he waited for his heart to burst.

Four or five times a week the chest pain came. His left shoulder would ache, and he would hyperventilate until the darkness moved.

His wife no longer listened to him when he claimed his heart was collapsing. She had sent him off to the doctor for a stress test, and he had crumbled into an anxiety attack as soon as the nurse had hooked him up.

Buttons attached, he had glanced at the jagged line of his heart, the pulse count numbers, everything red and green. The peaks and valleys looked regular; the red number said 70. And then it said 66, then 62, 59, 56, and Fetler felt himself dying right there in front of the nurse who looked to where he was pointing and saw 48, 45, 42. By this time Fetler was white and clammy and the last number he could focus on was 38. A few seconds later the doctor pulled the wires away and laid him back, pushing an ammonia capsule under his nose. There was nothing Fetler could do but lie there, humiliated.

What he had done, eventually, was take off his glasses so he could see nothing of the machinery. Ten minutes later he was able to joke about "choking on objective exams." The nurse wired him again, and he walked the treadmill with no difficulty.

For a week he had slept soundly, and then one night, after drinking beer for three hours, he was convinced he had killed himself, bolting up in bed for a last look at the world.

This uncle had been sixty-seven; his father had been sixty-three. There were six more in that generation, all of them between sixty and seventy. It would be a bust decade, full of these reunions that had last been formed by a cycle of marriages. In another ten years, Fetler and his brother and sister would watch their children disappear with some stranger, knowing the following decade would bring them back, two or three bored pre-teenagers straggling along.

Fetler pulled up in front of Ogrodnick's Funeral Home at quarter to two. He had stopped for cheese-

burgers, timing his drive so he would not arrive awkwardly late or early. He did not want to mumble condo-
lences to his aunt and then be trapped for fifteen minutes
of conversation. Better to step away almost at once,
using the ceremony as an excuse for brevity.

It was Aunt Mildred this time. She stood beside
Fetler's mother. He stepped up and placed his hands on
hers, leaned forward and kissed her cheek. It was easier
than speaking. "Thank you," she said. His mother whis-
pered, "You look tired."

"Long drive," he answered, something he had thought
to say while sitting in Wendy's.

When he was nine, she had taught him to say "My
sympathy" to great-aunts and great-uncles. He had been
speechless before the surviving grandparents. This time
he had left his own children at home. He used the im-
portance of their not missing school as an excuse, forcing
Carol to stay with them. He had two days without the
family, could run those into the weekend and stay for
two more.

A man he did not recognize moved toward his aunt
and Fetler was released. "Talk to you afterward," he said
to his mother, taking a few steps toward the casket,
pausing for a moment, and then finding a seat to the
side. He looked around for his sister. She sat on the aisle
with her husband. Her three daughters were all in dark
blue. His brother, he knew, would not be there, caught
in Chicago by a late-winter storm that was putting the
Great Lakes region out of business. The room seemed to
be dominated by women.

Untouched. He thought of his escape again during the
minister's message. A week before someone his age had

hit an ice patch on the road into town and had slid sideways into an oncoming bus. They had used something
called "The Jaws of Life" to extract his body from the car.
It had taken almost an hour to discover that his chest and
head had been equally destroyed. "These things are in-
evitable," the minister said. "We must recognize our
limits and accept that a well-lived life can lead to something greater than we know."

Fetler decided that he was going to sell the
Volkswagen. It was ten years old. It had never, despite
its reliability, handled well.

Ogrodnick himself placed Fetler in the procession.
Fetler was surprised. Ogrodnick was in his seventies,
had been doing the Fetlers for almost fifty years. He had
been ill when Fetler's father had died; an associate,
someone younger than Fetler, had been in charge, and
the change had made the funeral seem somehow like a
rehearsal.

Now Fetler sat beside his mother as they drove up
Sharp's Hill to the cemetery. Etna fell away behind
them, not one Fetler left in the borough although they
returned for funerals. "Carol's fine?" she asked.

"Uh-huh."

"The children?"

"Sure."

"It's a hard time here," she said. "You know that Karl's
had bypass."

"Yeah."

"And I'm back on medication."

"That's not so bad."

"No, not so bad. Better than the knife."

"Uh-huh."

"You know, if they ever put me under a general, I'll never wake up."

"Maybe the medication will be enough."

"Maybe."

They were quiet a moment. There was a difficult turn in the road, the kind of acute angle a bus would not be able to make in one swing.

"It has to be. I'll never wake up. I know it. Did you take a good look at Frank?"

He did not know what she intended. "Pretty good," he tried.

"No warning. And he was the one who didn't need a doctor. Just like that. No warning."

"So maybe it's better to be seeing someone regularly."

"But they can't put me under."

"What can you do by worrying?" It sounded so lame. Already he was thinking of how tight his chest felt.

*   *   *   *   *   *   *   *

From thirty feet away, Fetler was able to stare at Janet Matthews without her noticing. For twenty years he had been thinking of her every time he imagined that high school had been exciting or might somehow be altered. She had married the boy who had taken her out the Saturday after Fetler had thrown up a bottle of Thunderbird wine in her father's car.

It was Janet who walked directly toward him after the graveside service. She was smiling. She put her hands out and he covered them. "What kind of man hides behind a beard?" she said.

Fetler could think of nothing but spending the rest of his life with her. He began to imagine that the day's events had been full of secret meanings, that there was resurrection in everything he had done. Her father had been a close friend of his Uncle Frank; she had returned to Pittsburgh for a position in music at the university.

While his mother had made dinner, Fetler had to talk with his sister. "You look like Buddy Holly with those glasses," she said.

"Kurt Rambis," Fetler said.

"When did you stop wearing contacts?"

"You don't know Kurt Rambis."

"He's probably some guy who does Buddy Holly imitations, like those guys who get plastic surgery to look like Elvis."

"No," Fetler said, but his sister was staring at him.

"Your prescription's too strong to wear those glasses. The lenses make part of your face bend out of shape with the rest of it."

Fetler listened to his mother setting the table. "Do you remember Charley Rogers?" he said.

"He's somebody else who wore Buddy Holly glasses," his sister said.

"He was a legend."

"Really. What did he sing?"

"He went to high school with you. He was right in between us, a junior when you were a senior."

"I missed him."

"He wrestled a bear that year." She looked at him and he felt his eye sockets curving in as if refraction were real. "He won," Fetler added.

"So?"

"Think of it. A bear. You're seventeen years old and you've pinned a bear."

"So tell me, who's Kurt Rambis?"

His mother was opening the oven. Fetler pushed his glasses up higher on his nose. "He used to bet guys he could drink a can of beer faster than they could peel open the snap-top."

"That's why Kurt Rambis is famous?"

"Charley Rogers. And he won the bets."

"Nobody can do that."

"Remember snap-tops when they first came out? You had to pry them like a pistachio nut."

"You still couldn't win that bet," his sister said.

"Charlie Rogers did."

"There was a trick."

"That's what some guy said one night. He said Charlie was throwing the beer over his shoulder and not really drinking it." Fetler paused. His sister was looking out the window to where her daughters were playing with her husband. "So he said for the guy to stand behind him so he could check on it and when the guy stood there and the race started, Charlie just threw the beer in his face and said 'You're right. I throw the beer over my shoulder.'"

"I'm going to have to call the girls in for dinner so they're not all overheated."

"How could you not remember Charlie Rogers? I told you that story about the beer when we were in high school."

"I've got one for you," she said. "What song was Number One the week that Charlie Rogers threw the beer over his shoulder?"

"Are you serious?" Fetler said.

"You don't know," she said and went into the kitchen.

*   *   *   *   *   *   *   *

As soon as dinner was over, Fetler drove to Anderson Road and waited outside Janet Matthew's house like a high schooler. He tried to think of five minutes worth of interesting talk. While he practiced, Janet stepped outside and walked across the lawn.

"You could have come in for a minute," she said, getting in. "Nobody's angry anymore."

"I know," he said. He started the car at once and drove away from the city.

It turned out, she told him a little stiffly, that Michael had never grown, that despite college and a job, he was someone she had fallen in love with, not someone to live with. Fetler nodded and was glad, remembering Michael dancing with her as he slouched against a gym wall, slightly drunk. "I've thought about you," she said. He waited. "Really," she added, and he tried to match his expression to her intention. "I think quite a lot about music and how each performance is lost."

"I think we should stop at the first motel we come to," Fetler said, "because that's what I've thought about for twenty years."

She did not answer, and Fetler imagined her subtly moving closer to her door. "But everything else about me has grown since then," he said.

He thought she smiled. He pulled into the lot of a Howard Johnson's at the turnpike exit and looked at her.

"I have thought of you," she said. "I remember that you watched me after Michael. For the whole year you watched me."

He got out of the car and she followed, and after he got a key he was afraid to say anything to her so he kissed her and immediately undressed her, and, terrified, moved his hands slowly over every part of her body.

Later, he was able to speak. He said he wanted to hear her play. She moved her fingers lightly over him. He shivered and thought at once that everything they were doing was as lost as that music.

"What will you be doing a year from now?" she asked.

"Who knows?"

"Are you sure?"

"No."

"That's why things are sad."

It was then that Fetler knew he wanted her to become pregnant. He saw the child, a girl, growing up into a replica of her mother. He had thought of a thousand stories to tell her, but when her fingers touched him again they were replaced by one involuntary gesture, his hand lifting, unsure, and he was certain she saw him as sixteen—weak, defensive, all desire.

*   *   *   *   *   *   *   *

The year John Glenn had ridden into orbit, Fetler had touched her for the last time. After his humiliating night, he had called her about a dance the next Saturday. She had refused, and the following week everyone in his chemistry class had filed to the auditorium to watch the launch on one of the dozen sets scattered in the aisles.

Fetler had slipped into the boy's room, had combed his hair beside a couple of thugs stealing time from metal shop, and had gone right back to the classroom and the physics class project radio, tuning it to WAMO, the only station in Pittsburgh not covering the flight. The deejay talked about hair-straighteners; he played a song by Paul Peek called "Brother-in-Law (He's a Moocher)"; he played the Bluebells' big hit "I Sold My Heart to the Junkman," an ad for Tiger Rose wine, Gene and Wendell's "The Roach," the Vibrations' "Continental With Me, Baby" . . .

It was the same month Fetler had played backup for the Skyliners when they sang at the high school winter carnival. They had been slipping for a couple of years; they had not hit since "Pennies From Heaven." He sat behind them holding his saxophone and thought they looked a little like the hoodlums who made him circle the parking lot, and that girl singer who soared through every high note teased her hair into one of those sprayed beehives that said she would open any car door if the radio was playing.

He believed that. He remembered that a local girl named C. C. Joy had done the warmup act as "an unannounced guest," and that no one could have helped her take those catcalls from the dark.

The disc jockey emcee was a fat man named Rod. There had been more hoots, suggestive one-liners until the Skyliners had shut everyone up. The music had been simple. Fetler and the rest of the dance band had run through it one time with the director and laughed about it, but when the last chorus of "Since I Don't Have You" began, Fetler had stopped playing, listening to what he knew would be their final song, what they still got dates for, Number One three years before, that ending, those "you-oos" that built until every transistor nerve of him listened through his skin, knowing for sure he would believe every word when he sang it to himself at forty.

Instead of talking, he stared at her. She was not un-comfortable. He nudged the sheet down over her thighs.

"You're still jealous," she said.

"You're still the same."

She laughed. "How would you know?"

"You are. I'm sure of it."

She looked at him seriously. "It's having no children. You get to keep something in trade."

"You should know," he said, "that I've never touched another woman since I've married."

She leaned toward him as if searching for the reason for his confession. "Thank you," she said. Then, "You must be happy."

"No." He said it immediately, and she leaned closer.

"You have your sons."

"Both of them are bright," he said, and felt vulnerable, thinking that what he said sounded defensive.

"Like their father." He noticed the fine creases in her skin near her mouth and eyes. "The most intelligent in our class," she said. When he did not answer, she added, "You were voted that, remember?"

"It was a tie. Bill Griess tied me. He went to MIT."

"So unlike you, he was," she said.

Fetler was not certain of her reference. He reached for her again, sure of his hands this time.

*   *   *   *   *   *   *   *

He sat up as soon as he woke. Although there was no pain, he knew that it would follow in a minute, clamping down on his chest. Quiet, as if he were at home again,

Fetler sat on the edge of the motel bed and listened to his heart spattering at his wrists, his temples. Now that he had finished one old story, he recognized that this suffering he did was ridiculous and incurable.

Janet slept on her stomach, her face so deep in the pillow he imagined her suffocating. She was sprawled at an angle so her legs took part of his space while he sat there in the half light from the parking lot.

The pain dug into his shoulder. He thought he was holding his breath and found himself gulping air. He did not want Janet to wake.

Walking was best. He spent ten minutes pacing until he felt light and unstable, as if he were moving after three days of flu. It was the end of the attack. Janet had not stirred. Watching her sleep, he was positive she would live to be ninety, one of those wiry women who outlive their nieces and nephews and remember their men by a peculiar gesture or a pair of shoes they wore for too long, unable to let go of something comfortable.

The Aqua-Velva Man

I always had to have the last say. Preferably something ironic and biting. When I thought people deserved to suffer, I had to beat them with sarcasm, but for years, at least, I'd known when enough was enough. When to shut up. When to yell over my shoulder as I walked through a door or stepped into a waiting car. The older I'd gotten, though, the more often I'd found myself keeping at it like some yapping dog that won't give its yammering a rest even when you pull your foot back.

And then Mel Crawley said he would show me how to box because anybody with a mouth like mine had better learn how to use his fists. "Pretty soon you'll have no face," he explained. "One of these days your nose will be sideways, your teeth will be in the street, and your eyes will be so swollen shut you won't even be able to find what you've lost."

I had to admit I'd been picking lethal targets lately. Like the bouncer at the Smoke House who said my just-turned-21 ID was fake. I asked him how the IQ retest had gone, whether the review course had helped any. Like the big center for Steel Car who was carrying a gut now, but was six-foot-six, two hundred and sixty pounds, one of those guys with forearms so huge you didn't have to check the rest of him to estimate how easily he could snap your neck.

We'd lined up for free throws after I'd grabbed a fast-breaking guard from behind, not even pretending to be going for the ball. I was beat. It was the fourth quarter, and I'd been training at the Pizza Tavern, which sponsored the team I played for in the Mercer County Industrial League. I was leaning over, tugging my shorts and thinking about the evils of beer, when I heard "You cheap-shot again and you'll eat these elbows."

I watched the first free throw clank off the back rim while the goon-squad spokesman breathed near my ear. "The Missing Link Pivotman," I said. "Lucy's in a museum. You're too late to get laid."

"Asshole," he summarized, so I skipped blocking out, but the second shot swished and I looked like somebody who was hustling to get the break going, somebody who was upcourt early to beat his man for the easy hoop.

Anybody could have given me lessons—I'd never landed a punch in my life—but Mel backed up his offer by telling me he'd been boxing since he was ten years old, that his father, seeing he was going to be big, insisted that he learn. "Somebody's always going to want your ass," he'd explained.

I saw the sense of it. The gunslinger analogy. Certainly, I was wishing I'd had ten years of boxing behind me instead of a decade of woofing and bullshitting. I was taller than Mel. I had reach on him, and he only outweighed me by twenty pounds, but I felt like Stick-Man when we'd put on the gloves.

"Go ahead," Mel said. "Try to hit me."

It seemed like an easy lesson, Mel just backing off a step or moving to the side, gloves up and taking all of my half-hearted punches. I was lost. I was ready to acknowledge my futility because I couldn't imagine any motivation but terror or rage that would unleash my fists.

"You ready to block now?" Mel said, and I nodded, trying to mimic what I'd seen him do. I didn't even see the first hook. I hadn't thought about somebody using his left hand for anything but jabs and defense.

I wanted to say "Hold it"; I wanted to think about the consequences of rote learning for head blows, but Mel pounded me, maybe twenty shots, before he backed off.

I'd forgotten about holding up my hands in any way that looked like a boxer. I'd thrown my right arm in front of my eyes like somebody who didn't want to be splashed in a swimming pool; I'd bent my left arm in front of my stomach, so I'd taken those twenty punches like the class narc who'd told the teacher the school bully was smoking during recess. There was a dog whistle in my head. I was afraid to shake the cobwebs out because I was certain their intricate networks were all that was holding my brain in place. "You can't close your eyes like that," Mel said. "You can't hold your hands like that and expect to live."

I considered his advice while I tried to figure out how to get the gloves off without his help. I wanted to say something interesting and settled for "Fuck this," shaking the loose-laced mittens down until one slipped off and I could toss the other one across the room.

That year we were living in a house shaped like a motel—twenty rooms, ten facing ten along two halls that met at the crotch of a v. The college, unwilling to invest in another full-scale dorm, had built a barracks and called it upperclass housing.

It wasn't so bad. We had some slack because the house was a quarter mile from campus. The guy I lived with went home every weekend; across the hall was Mel's room, and his roommate had practically moved in with his girlfriend downtown. Tom Mayhall, who'd thrown up in his room twenty times during the first semester, lived next to me. He didn't have a roommate. Tom Mayhall had wrecked his Corvette during Christmas break, thrown clear instead of into any one of the trees that could have split his head. He walked with a limp now; he was supposed to exercise—stretch and strengthen—but he might as well have been told to drink a quart of milk a day.

Tom Mayhall lived on pepperoni pizza, hoagies, and bottles of wine; though one Friday, when he was looking for a nightcap, everyone else tapped out, I watched him drink a bottle of Aqua-Velva Shaving Lotion.

"There's something about an Aqua-Velva Man," he said after he'd chugged a month's worth of skin conditioner. He held up the bottle as if he were doing a commercial for lunacy.

He'd sold me. I thought you might die for this sort of foolishness, or at least go blind, but Tom Mayhall, an hour later, just threw up on the other side of the wall as if he'd tossed down another bottle of White Port.

I couldn't see myself getting that drunk. I thought I'd be the unlucky jerk who aspirated, strangling on fragments of Big Macs and French fries. I thought I'd mouth off to some off-duty bodyguard and forget I had legs. I was afraid of flopping behind the wheel of a car like the idiots who had skeletons superimposed on their bodies in public-service commercials.

I'd gotten my father's Mercury up to one hundred once, just so I didn't have to lie to say I'd done it, and then I'd slowed down and driven home, shaken, at fifty, turning off the radio because the music sounded like it was being amplified through a storm sewer. I'd driven that two-lane straight stretch twenty times since then and never once passed fifty-five. Each time I couldn't imagine how I hadn't panicked and jammed on the brakes, sliding the car into the guardrails, up and over and tumbling in a great barrel roll to extinction.

I was nervous just riding in cars driven by anyone else. Even at the speed limit I'd be checking the highway, looking for fools with no peripheral vision, with night blindness. Or just the stupid and the drunk.

I'd ridden, once, with Tom Mayhall, catching a ride to the middle school gym where Pizza Tavern had a game with Reynolds Aluminum. Mayhall had bought a Thunderbird by then. Some vintage year model, late 50s, I thought, expecting Mayhall to be taking driving more seriously after dodging death and investing a second tuition payment in a car. After all, we were only going across town, the speed limit thirty-five the whole way, but Mayhall had the Thunderbird up to seventy on the only half mile without a stop sign or a red light.

I had maybe ten seconds to get my life in order, and I used them to stare at Tom Mayhall. I thought he would look possessed, a drivers ed. version of depravity, his head thrown back, his mouth open for a huge howl at the heavens, but he didn't appear any different than my father as he took us down a back street paved with bricks and slid that Thunderbird through two right-angle turns.

Near the end of February, though, Tom Mayhall started playing "Nowhere to Run" in his room one night, listening for something I wasn't hearing because he'd replayed it eight times when I tried to get in his room to shut it off. His door was locked, and he yelled, when the arm was switching back to start Martha and the Vandellas over again, that he was eating aspirin until he died, that he was at twelve and counting. "Sure," I said. "Waste yourself, but shut that shit off."

No luck. The drum riff opened the vocal again. "Fourteen," he shouted. "Sixteen," he slurred, and I wanted to kill him myself to shut up Martha Reeves.

"Nowhere to hide . . ." the Vandellas chorused. "Eighteen," Tom Mayhall said. "Twenty."

I wanted Mayhall chewing Motown's vinyl, but at thirty-six Mel Crawley popped the lock with a credit card and was first in the room to assess how things stood. Mayhall burbled "Welcome," and Mel pulled the plug, slurping the suicide note to a stop. While I was turning my brain back to Def-Con One, Mel picked up the aspirin bottle from the floor where it stood beside a quart of Tiger Rose. "What the fuck?" Mayhall said, but Mel was counting tablets, pouring all of them onto the bed and lining them up by ranks of ten.

"Eighty-two," Mel finally announced. "You've been putting us on. You've been double-counting."

"What's it to you?" Mayhall said. "What the fuck any business is it of yours?"

I was ready to agree. "Give him the aspirin," I suggested, "but take the record with you."

But Mel wasn't through. "What about the eighteen?" he said. "Are those real?" I wondered how many times Mel would thump Tom Mayhall in order to teach him to survive, but Mayhall threw up then, heaved over the side of the bed, so I could leave both of them behind and maintain a silent conscience.

It was snowing outside. I could see exhaust escaping from three of the parked cars in the lot, the heaters running for the couples busy on their seats. I knew you could die, intentional or not, in idling cars, that all of those lovers were carelessly panting. Tom Mayhall had better sense than they did.

To get the edge off, I went downstairs to do some repetitions with the free weights the house had chipped in for the year before. I'd kept my vow to avoid boxing, but I hadn't been smart enough to give up weightlifting, even after I'd nearly strangled myself with a barbell.

I'd been lifting since the beginning of the semester, mostly bench presses and curls, trying to bulk up the parts of me that showed. Three or four guys in the house did fast reps of curls before they went out on dates, puffing their biceps. "How long does it last?" I always asked, and they'd say "Long enough," whatever that meant, though I gave up believing in that sleight-of-hand when I walked in on Ed Dunmire, who was engaged, doing reps before his date with a girl who'd been running her hands over his body for two years.

I was in for the long haul. I'd wanted to bench press 200 pounds because that was the first round number greater than my weight. I'd said "Yes" when the barbell dropped back into the rack above my head, but then I'd got to thinking about the possibilities of weight lifting, what 250 pounds would feel like, what I'd look like when something that outweighed me by nearly 60 pounds slammed into that rack.

Two weeks later I was trying 215 five minutes after I'd popped 210 for the first time. What was five more pounds? Mel Crawley said "Ready?" He was eating an apple while he was spotting for me, looking like he expected me to handle another personal best. I started to bring the weight down, touched it to my chest, and recognized immediately that I couldn't raise it, not even with one of those half-assed struggles, the right side of the bar higher than the left because I'd spent my whole life refusing to risk developing my weaker side. I couldn't even shoot a lay-up left handed, and I couldn't budge 215 pounds with both hands and the beginnings of prayer.

The bar slipped into the cradle of my throat. I was pushing as hard as I could to keep breathing. "Trouble?" Mel said, though unless you were in another room the answer was clear. He leaned over and watched as I did my survival isometrics. "Shows how easy it is to screw up eternally," he offered. "Never bench press without a spotter."

"Christ," I managed to exhale, and he stuck the apple in his mouth, gripped it with his teeth, and reached, finally, for the bar, lifting it enough to get things going again.

"You were looking lame there," he said, which convinced me I'd never lift another pound with Mel Crawley in the room.

Since then I'd picked times to work out when nobody would walk in on me. Mornings mostly. Especially Sunday. As long as Mel wasn't in the room, I could do repetitions on the bench without a spotter—150s, 160s,

170s—weights I could handle if I reached four and got the quivers.

I had enough adrenalin from Tom Mayhall's bout with the blues to start with 170, I thought, and I was right, managing three sets of five, feeling like it was time to show some serious progress. I slid tens onto each side; I tightened the screws and lay back on the bench to do a set of 190s.

I brought the bar down and pushed it up. I lowered it again, shaking some on the return trip, so I knew I wasn't going to finish five. One more then, I said to myself, allowing the bar to descend and confirming the existence of *déjà vu*. I even glanced up for a second to where Mel Crawley would have been, but I might as well have been looking for the extended hand of Zeus.

The 190 felt as exactly immovable as the 215. I thought about tipping the weights and taking my chances with throwing myself to one side before a set of plates crushed my skull. I considered screaming. And then I started rolling the bar down my body as if I'd volunteered to be a road bed.

When I passed my rib cage, I was pretty certain I was about to do myself some permanent harm. I tightened my stomach muscles and concentrated on a picture I'd seen, once, of a man who caught cannonballs with his gut for a living. Frank Richards, I remembered, was his name, coming up with something totally worthless under stress instead of praying for my pelvis and my thigh muscles.

And then I could sit up, and I had that bar on the bench, understanding at once that I could never mention this to anyone.

The next Saturday night Tom Mayhall was looking for the keys to his Thunderbird. He wanted to drive. He had a girlfriend who lived five miles from where he was standing. He'd had a bad night with her, and now he wanted to repent or else slap her around.

Tom Mayhall was drunk enough that I would have passed him the bottle if he'd asked for a swig of my English Leather. "Who took my goddamned keys?" he shouted each time he reeled through the foyer where the two hallways emptied. He'd been out to the car and back; he'd been through every drawer in his room twice, and I estimated two more trips before he'd throw up and fall asleep, waking tomorrow to discover the keys under his car or in the pocket of the jacket he'd been wearing before a half gallon of Boone's Farm Apple had turned him senile.

Ten more minutes, maybe, but then Mel Crawley walked upstairs from the television lounge and said, "I have your keys," holding them up in front of Tom Mayhall so I knew he wasn't just poking a stick through the bars.

"I want my keys," Mayhall said. He wasn't seeing Mel's theft as a sign of friendship.

Mel the Samaritan dropped them back in his pocket. "No," he said.

"Give me the fucking keys."

"Go to bed," Mel said in his best wise man's voice. "You'll thank me in the morning."

I was looking for the cameras. I was listening for someone to say "That's a wrap," but Mayhall was weighing his chances with Mel, whether or not he could be persuaded or thrashed.

I wanted to suggest "Keep your hands up; don't close your eyes," but Mayhall, instead of flailing away, said, "I'll be back in a minute" without looking like he intended to vomit his way into fighting shape.

He had another option. He kept an arsenal in his room, two rifles and a shotgun he'd brought into the TV room one night in October, explaining how he was ready if "the assholes tried to take over the country."

Mel Crawley had heard his guns-are-power monologue. He'd seen the bullet holes in the sign that said "Speed Bump" which the college had put up after a physical plant crew had poured a ridge of asphalt across the street a 100 yards from the house. Right away, Mel said "Hold it" and stepped in front of Mayhall.

"I'll only be a minute," Mayhall said. "I have to get something from my room."

Mel positioned himself in the hall doorway. "Not now," he said.

"It's my fucking room."

"Not anymore. Not tonight."

"I only need one thing."

Mel backed up then, retreating down the hall, and Mayhall followed him. "All right," Mel said. "Just wait a second."

"One thing," Mayhall repeated. "One little thing," and I watched from the end of the hall as Mel backed past our doors, stopped at Mayhall's door, opened it, thumbed the push-button lock from behind, and slammed it shut.

"Ok," Mel said. "You can go in now."

"What the fuck?" Mayhall queried. "What the fucking fuck?"

I started calculating the odds on Mayhall sorting through the apple wine to the memory of the credit card pass key, and I thought Mel was better than even money to live through the night. When Mayhall, instead of throwing himself at Mel's throat, walked back to his car and returned with a spare bottle of Boone's Farm instead of a pistol, Mel soared to prohibitive favorite.

Two hours later, turning out the light on another dodged-crisis evening, I figured Tom Mayhall for passed out somewhere, his car and his girl friend better off for it, but I hadn't been lying in darkness five minutes before I heard glass break.

I wasted too much time thinking about reasons for somebody smashing a window. I sat up in my bed and waited for what came next like somebody who relied on a butler to bring him common sense. By the time I decided to lock my door, it was already open. Someone was framed in the doorway. Someone was looking my way and breathing hard and making up his mind about how the next few seconds would unravel.

"Mel?" Tom Mayhall said, his hands coming up in front of him so I couldn't see whether or not he was kneading his wine cramps or leveling a gun.

"Don," I said at once. "I'm Don," I double checked. "You're in the wrong room," I kept on, hoping my voice sounded exactly the same as it had every time I'd spoken to Tom Mayhall. "Turn on the light. You'll see. Mel's not in this room," thinking, as soon as I paused, that directions were stupid, that my chance was sliding off the bed in the dark and diving underneath, hoping Tom Mayhall's rage was limited to firing at where my voice had been.

"Yeah," he said. But he didn't leave just yet. He kept his hands in the shadow of his body, trying to sort out, perhaps, the difficulties of left and right, having trouble seeing his way to correcting his mistake.

I told myself I wasn't going to explain the coin flip nature of his choice. If Mayhall was going to slaughter Mel Crawley, he'd have to choose the proper door on his own. And then he said "Sorry" and turned, and I could see he really did have a rifle, that Mel's door, incredibly, was unlocked, because Mayhall turned the knob and pushed it open, stepping forward and saying "Mel?" while he brought his hands up so I could see how he would have looked in my doorway if I'd been caddying for his vigilante tournament.

"Mel?" he said again, and I leaned forward, watching him disappear into the darkness, hearing him rustle through both beds, open and shut both closets. Mel wasn't there. Apparently, he'd been thinking more than I had, finding a suitable place to survive the night.

I pulled back a bit when Mayhall reappeared, but he moved down the hall toward the foyer. I waited another minute, my instincts still sputtering, and then stood up, finally, to go lock the door.

I was two steps into no-man's land when I heard a shot. I didn't have any reasons for substituting a firecracker or a back-firing car: the shot had come from outside, and I wondered if maybe Mel hadn't been clever, had just gone out for a late pizza and walked right up the sidewalk to where Tom Mayhall was waiting for revenge.

I looked out the window. For all I knew, Mayhall would shoot at shadows, but I was stupid with apprehension. It turned out Mayhall was on the side porch. If I leaned forward, I could make him out. Other than him, nobody seemed to be outside. There weren't any bodies lying in the snow or sprawled in the parking lot, so if he'd fired at Mel, he hadn't been lethal or he'd picked him off out by the speed bump.

I didn't have time to make any more guesses because Mayhall raised the rifle, sighted, and fired before I thought to drop to the floor. When I hoisted myself up again, the landscape looked the same. I didn't know what to make of it; Mayhall's night vision was way beyond mine.

All it was, was darker. Clouds had moved in, I deducted, but empirical evidence, at last, took over, and I followed the sight line to where Mayhall was pointing his rifle and saw he was taking out the street lights in the parking lot, that two of the six were already dark.

He fired again, and I witnessed a bulb explosion, watched its glass shower into the banked snow. Tom Mayhall was accurate. There wasn't much question he could shoot that rifle, so maybe he could have driven his Thunderbird, even thirty miles an hour over the speed limit. Maybe he could have arrived safe and sound at his girl friend's house and said the right things to encourage forgiveness. He wasn't shooting like a regular puker; nobody who'd fallen down a flight of stairs or lurched into a wall would be shattering those targets. Soon he was six of six, and the lot was so dark anything could be happening out there among the cars.

A set of headlights drove toward us, skipping up and then down over the speed bump, turning directly at the house without blinking off so I knew it was a patrol car, the local police, because there was only the driver and he walked directly toward the porch as if he were coming to ask for directions.

Tom Mayhall was finished. He was back in his room moving things around, I guessed, to redecorate for normality. But before the policeman came down the hall, he'd brought his two rifles and his shotgun into my room, had set the false ceiling aside, balanced them on the beams above us, and slid into my roommate's bed, saying, "Don't worry, they don't know a thing," counting on me to keep my mouth shut like the kind of man who slapped on after-shave, confident that his fantasies would materialize while his face was smooth.

My Father Told Me

For three weeks, each time I've called my father, no one has answered. I've let it ring twenty times. I've counted because I want to be certain I can tell him how far I've gone to account for his bad ear, his arthritis. How long I've waited in case he was outside trying to fumble his house key into the lock, nervous because the phone was ringing as he crossed the front porch from the driveway.

Altogether, I've phoned seven times, once each on every night of the week, staggering the calls over the days from Thanksgiving to the middle of December. I can explain my system to him as well, that I haven't just called on three Monday evenings when he was playing dartball in his church league. Or three Wednesday nights when he was watching television at his brother Ted's apartment. But with each succeeding call, I've understood I was counting the rings the way a boxer, standing in a neutral corner, might be singing along with the referee, impatient for ten.

I blame the joy of twenty on my father. For the first forty years of my life, either in person or on the phone, I talked with my mother. And when she died last January, there we were, my father and I having to feel our way into dialogue. And a month later, when I took three days off work to help him rearrange his life, division of labor was the password that kept us moving silently through my visit.

My mother had kept all of the financial records, so I spent the first day working through the books while my father vacuumed the carpets and dusted furniture. Three hours after we started, my father stopped in the spare room and asked me if I wanted lunch. "Sure," I said. "Whatever you have." He returned with an American cheese sandwich and a cup of coffee, put them on the table, and left.

In the middle of the afternoon he stopped by again and picked up the dishes. "Well," he said, "we're getting along here, aren't we?"

My father had allowed my mother to die an old-fashioned, stay-at-home, natural death. No machinery. No hospital. No exotic drugs. Most likely she could have lived another year; probably another two; maybe another three, all of those thousand days as an invalid he would have cared for if either one of them could have put up with even one day of her not being able to stand up or walk.

She'd managed, on the day she died, to finish the crossword puzzle in the city newspaper. All the way to having the patience to look up "Orison," a six-letter word for "prayer"; and "alim," which turned out to be "a Turkish standard." Or maybe she simply knew that stumper from having worked ten thousand crosswords. No matter, I'd thought, when I found the folded paper beside the couch on the day before the funeral; it was the kind of definition a lousy puzzlemaker would resort to when he'd worked his way out of English words. What remained was the evidence that she'd solved it, that there was no chance she'd filled in the toughest six spaces by checking the solution in the next afternoon's paper.

Every December, as the year runs down, I play my Phil Spector Christmas Album and reread the January issues of *Life* that I've collected. The year-in-review specials mix well with The Crystals singing "Santa Claus Is Coming To Town," the fads and the recent dead sparkle when Darlene Love is shouting out "Winter Wonderland."

This year I start with the January, 1984, issue, the one I bought on Christmas Eve in Hollywood, Florida. I was wearing shorts and loading up on expensive delicatessen food to take back to the condominium my family was living in for the holidays. The Hitler Diaries. Wacky Wallwalkers. Boy George posing with his mother. I end up reading a page of quotations, stopping at one attributed to William Fears, telephone lineman of Mill Valley, CA: "There's nothing in space—Believe me, I'm positive of that. My father told me."

I think about Bill Fears, whether or not he's followed Voyager to Neptune, the January, 1990 issue; remember that I'd woken up on Christmas morning, 1983, to the worst Florida cold wave in fifty years. I'd driven my family down to the Keys, thinking it would be warmer, and we'd spent the afternoon shivering in the bleak fifty degree sunlight of a Northeast March. On my stereo, Bob B. Soxx and The Blue Jeans finish "Here Comes Santa Claus," are replaced by the voice of Phil Spector, the Wall-of-Sound producer delivering his early-60s, end-of-the-album soliloquy over a wash of "Silent Night."

"It is so difficult at this time to say words that would express feelings about the album to which you've just listened," Phil begins.

"Sure, Phil," my youngest son, who is twelve, says from the kitchen. I look up from the pictures of Buster Crabbe and Arthur Godfrey, two people who died in 1983.

"Of course, the biggest thanks goes to you," Phil insists, and my son, standing in the doorway now, says "Sure it does, Phil," as "Silent Night" swells louder. "What a cheesy record," he adds, though, since it's over anyway, I'm not going to argue with him.

On the second day at my father's, I went into the basement to see what needed to be packed and kept, packed and given away, or packed and dumped at the end of the driveway for the trash collector. "You decide," my father said. "I won't argue."

I kept pictures, books, souvenirs—anything somehow symbolic. I charity-boxed used clothes and appliances. And then I hauled two dozen cartons of carpet remnants, wrapping paper scraps, ribbon pieces, and a hundred thousand labels from products that had promoted some sort of refund offers.

Maybe 500 hundred General Mills cereal coupons. At least as many Betty Crocker boxtops and Planters' Peanuts vacuum-jar seals. An old RCA color television box full of miscellaneous wrappers. A Sears washing machine box full of sorted, rubber-banded coupons. I didn't check to see what my father might receive if he mailed all of them in or lugged bundles to the grocery store. Whatever it was, he'd never miss it. There were expiration dates from the 1970's, thousands of "must redeem by's" from the 1980's. I didn't want to tell my father to spend the rest of his life searching for "9's" among the decade digits.

In the eleven months since my mother died, my father has called twice. And neither time was I home. He called after twelve, and my wife answered, thinking it was the police inviting her to the morgue. Maybe he's living strange hours now. Maybe he thinks the rates are lower after midnight. Each time he simply said "Tell him his father called."

At work, last week, I had to entertain the man who'd been hired to speak at the library dedication. Because there were four million dollars on display, five thousand dollars had been set aside for a visiting poet, who, I gathered, was supposed to be dynamic, somebody who could put a figurative face on renovation, a tougher task than extolling a new building.

Five thousand dollars, it turned out, bought the Poet Laureate of the United States, a title the government stamps on someone every year or two to certify that poets could grow old gracefully and fulfill the guidelines followed by a committee. The library had ordered every book still in print by the guest speaker; a librarian had put them on display in the lobby a few days before the ceremony; a clerk had been told to open each of the books, page through them, and make sure the backs wouldn't crack if anyone happened to examine them. On her own she'd stamped various due dates on the inside-back-cover slips, signed fictitious names beside them. "I thought it was the right thing to do," she said.

My role didn't begin until the day after the ceremony. I was the designated host, shuffling the poet from scheduled meeting to scheduled meeting, keeping him busy with conversations until the head librarian drove him to the airport late in the afternoon. It turned out he had one deaf ear, and I had to pop up on his good side each time we walked to another building or else I was talking to stone.

"I remember which side because you have the same deaf ear as my father does," I told him after I'd mastered the position, falling in place on his left as we put the local writers' guild behind us.

The poet smiled, and I thought, at once, that I'd been mistaken, that his wordlessness was an acknowledgement of the stupidity and carelessness of somebody who had forgotten the simplest of choices again.

We didn't have far to walk, so I let silence push us back to the library. One of the tasks I had to steer him to was the signing of each of the fourteen books on the display shelves, and I looked out one of the thin, swept-upward contemporary windows in the new front wall of the renovated lobby while he labored his signature onto each title page. I didn't want to tell him that those signatures meant the books would be stored in Archives, that every autographed book in the library was automatically taken out of circulation. When he was nearly finished, I approached him from behind and said, "Two more interest groups to go." And when he turned left to find me, his smile matched up with the Mona Lisa's and Charles Starkweather's in my enigma scrapbook. The next time I call my father, I'll have at least one new story to tell him.

On the third day I stayed with my father, after breakfast, he said, "I want to show you something."

"What?"

"In the garage."

There was no point in saying "What?" again. It was maybe twenty degrees outside, maybe thirty in the garage, and I buttoned up my coat while waiting for him to choose from the floor-to-ceiling junk that surrounded us.

It had been five years, at least, since he'd squeezed a car in there, and finally, when he'd given it up, the room had narrowed rapidly to the width of a lawn mower. I felt, for a moment, like somebody whose job it was to rescue earthquake victims, reach among twisted metal and broken concrete for quivering or lifeless hands.

I was watching my breath while he moved a barrel that, for all I knew, held a million Cheese-Puff labels. "Here," he said. "Look."

It was a safe. For sure, I hadn't been expecting a safe. "You need to know the combination so you can get in here some day." He had me stumped. I didn't know what my father could have been hoarding that needed a combination lock to protect it.

"Ok," I agreed.

"Pay this some mind now."

"Ok," I repeated with brilliance.

"Right four times to forty; left three times to thirty; right two times to twenty; left once to ten; right to zero and bingo."

I thought he was kidding. I thought he was making sure I wasn't daydreaming about cutting the lawn with one of the three handmowers jammed against the back wall under a set of bedsprings.

"You got it?"

"No problem."

He gave the dial a spin. "Go ahead."

I decided to play it out, call his bluff. When I got back to zero, I tugged the door like I believed in my father's infallibility and the thing opened. "Good," he said. He pushed the door shut with his foot and respun the dial. "Now you know."

Phil Spector over with, I turn on the radio, an oldies station, and pick up *Life*, January, 1989, the issue I bought the day I got home from my mother's funeral.

Pictures of Roy Orbison, John Houseman, Billy Carter, Louise Nevelson—they'd died, for sure, before my mother, even Roy Orbison, who, as I remember, died just in time to make this issue.

On the radio, the announcer says, "Hello, Solid Gold Saturday Night—Who's this?"

"This is Bill," the caller answers, sounding oddly like my father.

"Where you calling from, Bill?"

"Pittsburgh," the caller replies, and I'm sitting up, listening, because so far it's a match of voice, name, and city.

"That's triple-W, S, right?"

"Right," Bill from Pittsburgh says, "WWSW." The call letters sound like they're being spoken by a seventy year-old man, somebody who would never call a syndicated rock-and-roll show.

"And what can we play for you, Bill?"

"'The Hippy, Hippy Shake.'"

"I can't stand still . . ." The Swinging Bluejeans begin, and I imagine my father listening to the recording of his call, thinking somehow the odds were good that I was simultaneously tuned in hundreds of miles away. Wasn't this my music? Hadn't I been glued to the radio all of the time when I was in high school?

Though of course there are thousands of Bills in Pittsburgh, dozens of them who would sound like my father on the radio. And one of them loved "The Hippy, Hippy Shake." And that particular Bill was holding a beer and dancing by himself in his living room, shouting through the house to his wife, saying "Listen to that, would you? Isn't it great?"

ABOUT THE BOOK

This book was designed by Allan Kornblum, and was set in Caslon and Estro types. The high resolution output was supplied by Hi Rez Studio. This book has been printed on acid-free paper, and has been smyth sewn for reading comfort and for added durability.